The Pistachio Seller

Middle East Literature in Translation

Michael Beard *and* Adnan Haydar, *Series Editors*

Syracuse University Press and the King Fahd Center for Middle East

and Islamic Studies, University of Arkansas, are pleased to announce

THE PISTACHIO SELLER *as the 2009 Winner*

of the King Fahd Center for Middle East and Islamic Studies

Translation of Arabic Literature Award

The Pistachio Seller

REEM BASSIOUNEY

Translated from the Arabic by Osman Nusairi

Syracuse University Press

English language edition copyright © 2009 by Syracuse University Press
Syracuse, New York 13244-5290

All Rights Reserved

First Edition 2009
09 10 11 12 13 14   6 5 4 3 2 1

Originally published as *Bai' al-fustuq* by Madbuly publishers in Cairo (2006).

∞ The paper used in this publication meets the minimum requirements
of American National Standard for Information Sciences—Permanence
of Paper for Printed Library Materials, ANSI Z39.48-1984.

For a listing of books published and distributed by Syracuse University Press,
visit our Web site at SyracuseUniversityPress.syr.edu.

ISBN-13: 978-0 8156-0919-3 (cloth)

Library of Congress Cataloging-in-Publication Data

Bassiouney, Reem.
[Ba'i' al-fustuq. English]
The pistachio seller / Reem Bassiouney ; translated from the Arabic by
Osman Nusairi. — 1st English language ed.
   p. cm. — (Middle East literature in translation)
ISBN 978-0-8156-0919-3 (cloth : alk. paper)
I. Nusairi, Osman.   II. Title.
PJ7816.A768B3513 2009
892.7'36—dc22   2009026110

Manufactured in the United States of America

To my parents, Nour El-Hoda and Ahmed Refaat.

You are always the first to read my work and to laugh and cry with my characters.

Egypt is now ready for pistachios.

—Wafaa

You can defeat reality with a lot of imagination.

—Anon.

REEM BASSIOUNEY was born in Alexandria, Egypt, in 1973. She graduated from Alexandria University, Faculty of Arts, English department. Since then she has taught in various universities including Alexandria University, University of Oxford, University of Cambridge, University of Utah, and Georgetown University. She was also a radio announcer in Egypt and a freelance journalist and writer.

She left Egypt at the age of twenty-three to study for her master's and doctoral degrees at Oxford. Before doing so she worked for two years as a lecturer at Alexandria University and taught at the branch of Alexandria university in Damanhour (a provincial town sixty miles from Alexandria, the place where most of *The Pistachio Seller* takes place). *The Pistachio Seller* has been voted the best novel of the year 2006 by *Al-Sharq al-Awsat* magazine and also by the International Alexandria library literary committee (2007).

Bassiouney is assistant professor at Georgetown University. She is the author of three other novels, *The Smell of the Sea* (2005), *Professor Hanaa* (2007) and *Love, Arab Style* (2009), as well as a number of short stories. Reem Bassiouney currently lives in Virginia with her husband and two children.

Contents

Acknowledgments

THANK YOU to all those who helped in this project directly or indirectly: to Michael Beard, whose friendship is one of the best gifts I got out of writing, and to Adnan Haydar, for his support and encouragement.

Thank you to all the readers who brighten my days with their e-mails and to all the critics who perhaps never met me but love my work nevertheless.

My thanks to D. J. Whyte for her wonderful editorial work, and to the staff at Syracuse University Press, who have both efficiency and a taste for literature. The cover designer, Lynn Hoppel, captured the essence of the work, and so did the others on the team, including Lisa Kuerbis, Marcia Hough, and Kay Steinmetz.

Thank you to Shahla Suleiman, a precious friend I was lucky and proud to acquire after she read this novel.

I extend my gratitude to the Egyptian author Gamal Al-Ghitany, whose vision and work open realms of discovery into the Egyptian identity and who was the first to publish my work in his literary magazine; to the acclaimed critic Dr. Salah Fadl, whose style captures the essence of life and who took the initiative in reviewing my first novel; and to Mary Selden Evans, a woman who impressed me on many levels and whose support helped immensely in this project. Such women create and maintain history.

The Journey

Imagination is more important than knowledge. For knowledge is limited to all we know and understand, while imagination embraces the entire world.

—Albert Einstein

1

HOW DOES A WOMAN fall in love?

When she sees a man from a different angle.

It was a Saturday. The electricity was out for two hours. When it came back on, most of the light bulbs in the hall were burned out. A main fuse in the apartment had also blown. My mother looked baffled; my brother was at a loss; even my father was at his wits' end. It was Ashraf who got up and volunteered to replace the fuse and the light bulbs.

He stood on the table. He was tall—very tall. His legs seemed to reach to the sky. He was tall and brown with a thin face and a smile like that of Ikhnaton. That tired and sarcastic smile seemed to say: I don't believe you, and I am fed up with your tricks, but I don't care.

Ashraf Daawood knew he was good-looking. There are men whose eyes shine with enough arrogance to mask the sunshine. His eyes needed no sunglasses, for arrogance was glittering and oozing from them.

My mother looked fondly at her nephew and said, "Have you always been an electrician?"

"No," he said, shaking his head, "but I like manual work."

Everyone watched him in silence.

It was a Saturday, I remember. And while he was standing on a stepladder in the hall, changing a light bulb in the faint light coming through the window, I decided to love him.

There was something about his white shirt, his jeans, his hand as I saw it in the dim light, the veins of his hand, that drew my attention to him for the first time. That was the beginning of my love story with Ashraf. When he stepped down from the ladder, he took a towel from his aunt and started wiping his hands. I was gazing at his hands and at the towel, and my heart was pounding like never before.

I looked at his trouser pocket, where he kept some pistachios. Two of them dropped to the floor, and the sound startled me. They were round and small. The first pistachio peeked cautiously from its shell. It was beautiful, and its green color revealed its innocence. The second pistachio looked pale and terrifying. It was as if it were counterfeit currency, antiquated laws, policies: democratic, capitalist, and radical all in one; it was like all subversive and arrogant ideas. It was as if it were the pain of days past and days to come. It was a cheap pistachio, as cheap as modern civilizations and as rotten as ancient ones. It was exorbitantly priced and of unknown origin. Was it originally from the East or the West? Was it from one of Ashraf's various countries? Or from the Zionists, the Americans, the Iraqis, the Syrians, the Iranians, the Turks, or the English?

It was a small, frightening pistachio, and as grave as death. Its mystery never left my imagination—just like the enigma of death. As for Ashraf Daawood, my love for him was succulent and violent.

Before that day, I had hated him passionately. Now everything had changed. I don't know why. I smiled shyly, since I didn't know what to do. Perhaps it was time to give my mother a hand. Yes, if I would do that, he was bound to see how good I was, and he would love me.

Heading for the kitchen, I called: "Mother, I'll do the washing up and then prepare dinner. Do you need anything else?"

My mother looked at me—as if she were aware of everything: "No, Wafaa, darling. Just make some coffee for Ashraf. It's time for his coffee, you know."

Making his coffee, I went damp with perspiration. I put the coffee down in front of him and sat looking at him. "Maybe I'm not in love with him," I thought. "Maybe. I don't know how to explain these strange feelings of mine. Maybe I just find him good-looking. No—there's a big problem for me here. I don't look at men. Then again, Ashraf is different."

I stared at the floor without uttering a word—while he was looking at me, rather surprised, and with a measure of curiosity. Then he said, "Wafaa, if you would like to study, do go to your room. I am no stranger."

"Yes. Certainly. I'll be going," I said hurriedly. I added, "but I have studied enough for today."

He held his cup of coffee, smiled, and said, "Thanks for the coffee, Wafaa. When you come and visit me in Cairo, I'll prepare lunch for you myself."

His words excited me. Once more I began to sweat as I was wringing my hands. I fixed my gaze on his hands while my imagination ran wild for a while: I felt his hand touching mine. He passed his hand over mine. He held my hand fast, began to stroke my arm, to stroke my . . .

The devil! The evil works of the devil! There I was imagining things no good girl from a good family like mine should imagine. From that day forward, I'd have to control what I thought. Yes—what if Ashraf found out about these evil fantasies of mine . . . or my mother? Oh, my God!

I rose hurriedly. My feelings were confusing and frightening. Was what I felt toward him love? Is that what love is like? And those devilish fantasies and dreams, what were they?

I went to my room. I did not go out to him again, but I never stopped dreaming.

The story began when Ashraf returned from Britain about thirteen years ago.

Cairo International Airport, 1980

"I pity airports. They are places that never become an end in themselves. They are exactly like visiting call girls. Who visits a call girl and stays with her? That doesn't mean I have ever visited a call girl. Why would I visit a call girl? And why would I stay?

"Who has ever had a yearning for an airport? Who among us does not feel bored while standing at the check-in counter or waiting for luggage?

"I once made a pledge that one day I would go to an airport as an end in itself. I would spend hours looking at advertisements and reading arrival and departure screens while talking with customs officers and staring at luggage. I would spend hours drinking tea and listening to the loudspeakers announcing departure times for various destinations."

This is what Ashraf was telling himself as he entered Cairo's International Airport from the airplane walkway. As for me, I have never left Egypt.

⌒

Ashraf looked at his British passport and then his Egyptian one. He thought, looking at both passports somewhat anxiously, "Now, which one do I need? Each age requires a different passport, and each country has a different feel."

What did he expect from Egypt? It was his country, although he had not lived there and did not know it. He had spent his childhood in a British boarding school, as his father had desired. He wanted Ashraf to be British, while his mother wanted him to be Egyptian. The disagreement between his parents had intensified and had taken the form of a strange conflict of civilizations, which he could not comprehend.

In British public schools he had learned how to be enchanting, how to bewitch those around him with his sweet words and bright smile. He had learned that showing anger in front of others was the equivalent of stripping naked in Trafalgar Square. Emotions do not establish a civilization; they kill it. He may have felt that he was better and more intelligent than others, but he had also learned to suppress his contempt of others, just as he had learned to suppress anger. At boarding school he had learned how to suppress his yearning for his mother. He had learned to become English, observing table manners and saying "please" and "thank you."

He had grown up during the era of the Conservative Party, and on the wealth of his father, a physician. His own wishes were modest: he wanted to be among the rich and to enjoy, in moderate terms, the pleasures of life.

He looked at the long line behind the sign reading "Non-Egyptians" and then at the shorter line behind the sign reading "Egyptians."

He hid his British passport in his pocket, pulled out the Egyptian one, and presented it to the immigration officer with a smile.

The man started writing down his passport details and asked, "Are you returning to settle permanently?"

He shook his head. "I will be working here for a British bank for only one year."

The officer returned the passport to him and gave him a routine welcome to Egypt.

Ashraf looked with boredom at the baggage on the conveyer belt in front of him. This was the moment he hated most: waiting for his luggage, which sometimes took hours.

Had Egypt changed?

Seven years earlier, he had come for a visit. He was then in his early twenties. He had taken a short trip with a friend to Luxor and stayed for two weeks with his mother's sister. The holiday was no longer than two weeks. It was just like a holiday in Cyprus, Greece, or Spain.

His mother had always told him that Egypt was where life keeps its secret essence. What *he* knew about Egypt was based on a book about the pharaohs that his mother had kept together with family photographs and the songs of Abdal-haleem Haafiz and of Umm Kulthoum, the famous Egyptian singers.

He feared for his mother. He could see her sinking into an unknown future, although he would rather not think about it right now. His relationship with her was a mixture of pity and suppressed love. As for his father, he admired his success but had no respect for his weakness toward women, nor did he comprehend it.

Taking his suitcase, he walked to the railroad station to take a train to Damanhour, where his aunt Manaal lived. He would stay there for about a week, until he found a place in Cairo, where he was to work as a financial expert for a British bank. He would work in Egypt as a Briton, not as an Egyptian.

He stepped off the train. So this was Damanhour: halfway between a city and a village. To the right of the station there were small overcrowded huts. In one of them a woman was washing clothes in a huge cooking pot; in another, someone was preparing sandwiches filled with cheese and liver of unknown provenance and with an unknown future. There was a man wearing a cotton vest sitting outside his hut and screaming at three of his children. There were children whose faces were covered in flies that would freely and safely commute between their eyes and mouths. Ashraf looked around him once more: to the left of the station, makeshift food stands covered the pavement. Here, a popular butcher would put the barbecue outside his shop to entice passers-by with the aroma of parsley and grilled meats from an unknown animal, just like the liver. There, the pastry maker offered all sorts of pies and pastries, as well as oil-soaked Egyptian pizza. The place was also teeming with sausages, peppers, and tomatoes, aged or rotten. He took another look at the vendors who sold everything: cooking pots, china sets, lipstick, kohl, hairpins, and red hearts that decorated a multitude of objects such as pillowcases and small teddy bears. He smiled sardonically; it seemed that love and flames were part and parcel of this town.

He hailed a taxi. As he was riding, he kept looking all around him. He saw busy streets, half-finished buildings, tall residential blocks and short ones, and signs on different apartments: *Dr. Nihaal Abdulla, Public Health, Slimming, and Diabetes Consultant* and *Dr. Ali As-salaami, Professor of Ear, Nose, and Throat Department.*

He took a deep breath. Inside the cab the air was filled with the odors of animal droppings and of old leather seats.

As he knocked on the door of his aunt's house, he tried to recall what the house looked like. All he could remember was the spacious living room, the table covered with a red lace cloth, and the cheap porcelain figurines displayed everywhere. He could also recall the gold-colored living room furniture and the giant chairs that, when he sat in them, gave him the feeling that they could swallow him up at any time.

A few minutes later he was gazing at his aunt, who was sitting on the right-hand side of the sofa. She was in her early forties and looked a lot younger than his mother. Her wavy hair screamed out her identity, as if saying, *I am from Damanhour. I belong to a woman who wraps and bands her hair, who tries every trick to straighten her curls.* However, a small curl undermined the attempt.

He looked at his uncle, who was sitting to the left of the sofa, with some space separating him from his wife. His features were exaggerated; his eyes were filled with both mockery and sarcasm. Ashraf understood the sarcasm to be directed against his wife's wavy hair.

Their son entered the room proudly. He sat in the middle of the sofa as if he were the man of the house, its pride and glory.

～

I entered. I was twenty years old at the time. I said to my brother, breathlessly and panting, like a dog following its owner, "Do you want anything to drink, Kareem? Anything to eat?"

When Sally entered I made my displeasure obvious, as usual. However, the pride showing in Sally's eyes—she was barely eighteen back then—enchanted Ashraf. No more than a few minutes had passed before he had decided that I was a model of backwardness and ignorance. On that day, the story of his hatred for me began.

～

Everyone was talking to him at once, nonstop. He just kept looking at their eyes. He could not work if they were under his spell, wanting something from him, finding him despicable, or all that rolled into one!

His uncle said in his quiet tone, "Ashraf, this is the right time for projects and enterprise. I have begun exporting textiles, praise be to God. What about you? Do you intend to work only in the bank? Are you going to settle here?"

Questions rained down on him—as if he were being interrogated about committing crimes against humanity or about his involvement in networks operating against democracy and human rights.

He tried to answer tersely. Then his aunt rose and called out enthusiastically, "Darling, I will make you a mango juice—my specialty."

If there was one thing Ashraf hated, it was mango juice squeezed in a house with dirty walls. He could not stand it even in his aunt's house. He was certain that his aunt would squeeze the mango with her fingers—and God knows where they had been. She would probably lick her fingers afterward or even wipe her nose—who would ever know? His arms had goose bumps as he looked at the juice.

Then he heard Sally, his young cousin, whisper, "Lucky you, Ashraf."

He smiled at her with curiosity. Sally looked around briefly, as if to ensure that no one was within earshot. "You live in Britain. In Britain, you have no brother like Kareem or sister like Wafaa. No one to say, 'No cinema for you, Sally' or 'You are not allowed to come home late, Sally.'"

He smiled rather cunningly and said, "I understand. You have grown up, cousin." For a brief moment she looked confused. Then she replied, "If you are asking whether I have a boyfriend, then—yes. But if you tell Wafaa she will tell Kareem, and if she tells Kareem he will beat me. If he does, I will leave home. Really, I will."

Ashraf asked, laughing, "And why would Wafaa tell Kareem?"

"Because Wafaa is mean and difficult. She has strange views. Please don't tell Wafaa what I told you, Ashraf."

"Of course not."

"Why don't you marry Wafaa? In spite of everything, she is good-hearted and very polite, though slightly boring."

He said, astonished, "Marry her? Without knowing her?"

She whispered, as if about to reveal something serious, "Everyone expects you to marry her. Mother hopes that you will do it. If she gets married, then I will be rid of her."

"And what about Wafaa?" he asked.

Indifferently, she said, "She cannot stand you. But that's not a problem. In old films cousins who can't stand each other get married and fall in love."

"Thank God for that," he replied, as if he had not heard her last sentence.

"She thinks you're a degenerate," she said before suddenly covering her mouth with her hands.

He merely looked at her inquiringly, "Wafaa thinks I am degenerate?"

She hastened to say, "Wafaa is a bit of an idiot. She listens to what Aunt Aliyya tells her. She is a rigid girl and really extremist."

He nodded as if he understood what she had said, though he did not know who Aunt Aliyya was—nor did he want to.

"You are just open-minded, and you enjoy your time. Lucky you, Ashraf. I wish I had been born in Britain."

It was then that his aunt Manaal entered. Thus began the torturous rites that would usually lead the prisoner to a full confession.

"You haven't had your juice, sweetheart. You must drink. On my life."

He knew he had to use all available weapons to fend off his aunt, especially as he had to stay with her for a whole week. If she intended to get him married to her daughter before the week was out, he would have to use all his reserves and emergency tactics. He said quickly, as he turned to his suitcase, "I have some small presents. Just a few little things."

"Oh, you should not have bothered, darling!"

He said nothing. He went for the suitcase and retrieved the presents that had been chosen by his mother.

"Ashraf, better drink the juice first; then we can look at the presents," his aunt said.

~

He reached inside the suitcase and pulled out a box of pistachios. He handed it over to my mother, who froze suddenly. I had entered the room carrying a huge onion that I had been about to cut.

"Mother, do you want a whole onion or only half?" I inquired before looking at the pistachios.

Sally was quick to comment, "Oh, my God, Mother, pistachios!"

Mother held fast to the box as if it were her treasure alone. "Everyone, take a bit. The rest we will keep for guests."

"Where are the pistachios from?" I asked.

Once more, I'd managed to establish that I was the embodiment of stupidity. Every word I uttered was further testimony.

"From Britain, Wafaa," he said.

"I mean, from where originally? They do not grow pistachios in Britain, do they?"

He shrugged indifferently. "I don't know where they are from."

Kareem entered and grabbed for the box. His mother surrendered it to him and said, "Don't eat it all by yourself, Kareemo. Leave a bit for your sisters. As I have told you, everything is to be shared by all of you." She then turned to Ashraf and said, "See? We're not into that thing of favoring boys."

Ashraf smiled sarcastically and said, "Of course not, Aunt Manaal. That's obvious."

~

Ashraf slept that night in the same room as Kareem. He was restless and somewhat disgusted. He had to tolerate his aunt and her children for a whole week.

The next day his aunt invited a family friend over. She meant to show off her nephew to the senior officer Midhat al-Awaisi. She cooked some stuffed cabbage drowned in ghee and the duck soup that she does so well. She heaped attention on the officer's wife, meeting all her wishes and bringing her juices, tea, and coffee.

Manaal sat proudly and said, "My darling Wafaa has helped me with the cooking today. The girl is very clever and energetic. She is doing well in her classes, too."

Ashraf was taking it all in with an admiring anticipation, as if watching a film in a language he did not understand. As he watched his aunt panting breathlessly before the officer's wife, he put on a tired and sarcastic smile.

He ignored his aunt and her obvious hints. He expected that she would suddenly ask him about the date of his marriage. He wished the week would be over as soon as possible.

∿

His only consolation was that I never liked or tolerated him, at first.

I had once chanced upon him coming from Kareem's room and asked, curious, "Ashraf, where do you suppose those pistachios came from? Israel?"

This seemed to have surprised him immensely. Suppressing a laugh, he said, "Why do you think that, Wafaa?"

"Because Europe trades with Israel more than it does with Arab countries. If nothing is written about their origin, then the pistachios are from Israel, prepared especially for Arabs in order to finish them off. Do you understand? Maybe radiation or poison of some sort or another," I said casually.

He heaved a deep sigh and said as he entered the living room, "No, Wafaa, I do not believe they grow pistachios there. They may be from Syria, Iran, or America, or all three. Do you hate Israel, Wafaa?"

"No! No—I don't hate Israel; we have a peace treaty with Israel. I don't hate it. I only fear it."

"Why?"

"I don't trust it."

He seemed to be tired of talking to me. He didn't understand me. To him, I represented everything he did not understand or accept.

∿

It was a sad day indeed when Ashraf met Lubna Thaabit and the story of their affair began—Ashraf, the pistachio man, with Lubna, the communist journalist who called for equality and liberty.

His story with me had also started, but I feared God and the torture reserved for sinners in their graves. I was terrified of God . . . and of my aunt Aliyya and my mother as well. I was simple and stupid. At the same time, my imagination was a wild beast, and I was unable to tame it. From time to time my imagination would assail me and ravish a piece of my flesh. It was all my imagination . . . and my love! When a woman is in love she does stupid things, as well as very dangerous ones. In fact, she may do some delicious things, too. That is when a woman is in love. She may also do nothing at all. She may give in to her imagination and feel guilty because of the filthy dreams that take hold of her. I often felt guilty because of the fantasies I had when I was with him, when I was with Ashraf Daawood. But I was afraid and stupid. My imagination used to make me totally senseless every now and then. It was a sad day for me when he set eyes on Lubna in Damanhour.

∿

I had not wanted to go out with him, but my mother had insisted. Of course, I knew that my mother wanted to find me a groom, and that she had set her cap for Ashraf in particular. He gave me a phony smile as he looked at me walking next to him with my brother toward the club in Damanhour.

He looked at me in my pink dress with its blue roses, at the hair covering my face, at my mascara-lined eyes, and at my red lipstick. I looked like the Moulid dolls he might have seen sold in the shops—fake, starched, and lifeless.

However, he did not reveal his feelings. He just asked, "How is school? Tell me about your university. You study archaeology, don't you?"

I nodded, blinking fast. Suddenly I felt terribly shy, tongue-tied. I didn't know why I should feel shy if I didn't love him. Women are shy only with the men they love and no others. Isn't that so? And I don't love deviants and degenerates like him. I knew that well.

Trying to shed my bashfulness, I ventured, "At university there are two, indeed three, types of girls."

"The first type being . . . ?"

My brother interrupted: "Here, Ashraf. This is it. Come on in."

He ignored him and repeated, "The first type?"

"The normal type, like me, for instance."

He smiled mockingly as he entered the club. "And what does the normal type do?"

I said spontaneously as I entered, "Studies, worships God, is good to her parents, and avoids whatever is suspicious."

"And what is considered suspicious in Egypt?"

"Men and politics."

He just laughed and walked with me into the club, while Kareem talked incessantly.

We sat together at a table that seemed to have suffered a lot of abuse. I sat like an obedient daughter or a diligent pupil, with my fingers interlaced in my lap, saying nothing.

My brother called out to the waiter, "We want tea and a *sahlab* drink. What about you, Ashraf?"

"Why didn't you ask your sister?"

"I know she wants tea."

"I'd like coffee," he said, smiling.

Ashraf was silent. He was, no doubt, altogether looking forward to the end of this day and this week.

Kareem said boisterously, "My father said you have come to work . . . to start a new project, a British business venture in Egypt. Father wants to export fabrics to Britain. Is that even possible?"

"Everything is possible, Kareem."

"And you will help us, of course," he said with the same zeal.

Ashraf turned his face to the next table. "Of course." He knew that in the eyes of his aunt, he was a Sinbad coming home with great treasures, with the power of lions and magic.

"How long will you stay here, Ashraf?"

"Maybe for a year—I don't know."

᷉

His eyes met hers. He had heard her voice traveling from the neighboring table. The voice was strong and deep. Lubna was shouting and puffing her cigarette at the same time, and he could not understand how. "This is my article. I want my name on it. Do you understand, Ali? I do not fear anyone! You know me, Ali!"

The man sitting opposite her said feebly, "Take it easy, Lubna—people are watching you!"

"It is my article! No name but mine should be on it!" Then she shouted, "My article! Enough of theft and plagiarism!"

Ashraf eyed her with astonishment and admiration. Her features were sharp and slight. She was short and tan. Her hair was coarse, and bound in a ponytail. She wore a tight pair of trousers. Her eyes were wide-open and daring. They seemed to take up the whole of her face. That face was bony and the cheeks wide. She looked like a painting done by a traditional painter. Her fingers were thin; they kept darting to and from her mouth.

A few minutes passed before Kareem, Ashraf, and some others intervened in the quarrel between Lubna and Ali. It also took just a few minutes for Ashraf to decide that he wanted her. He wanted this Lubna who was fighting everyone around her for reasons he did not know or comprehend. He just knew he wanted her.

❧

He turned his face toward me and asked suddenly, "And the second type?"

"Pardon?"

"The second type of woman?"

I gasped, disgusted. "The likes of that woman. The tomboy type who thinks she is like a man, who wants to change everything. The type of woman who gets into fights all the time even with the flies on her face. I bet she's into politics as well. You know, at the university there are rallies and demonstrations all the time. I don't know what they want. They just protest against anything and everything."

His eyes followed Lubna as she confidently headed toward the door. He was dazzled: I don't think he had ever seen a woman with such strength, either in Britain or elsewhere. The wild desire to draw her inside him showed on his face. It was a goal he wanted to achieve: Lubna Thaabit, the Egyptian journalist. He never forgot the name.

He said, as if suddenly remembering an address of a house he had forgotten for ten years, "What is the third type, Wafaa?"

I took a gulp and said contemptuously, "The corrupt girls living in the female students' dormitory. Do you know why Father didn't consent to my staying in the girls' dormitory?"

"Why?"

"You don't know anything. Some girls there . . ." I fell silent, embarrassed.

So he asked, "What do they do, Wafaa?"

"I cannot tell you."

He smiled. Maybe he'd admit to himself that I was extremely amusing, to an extent he had not imagined.

He asked again, "What do they do, Wafaa? Befriend men?"

I nodded.

"And what else?"

"They go in cars with men," I said, without looking at him.

But he merely laughed. "Really?"

"Yes, believe me. Just like Western girls. Some of them smoke, like the girl we just saw. Ashraf, don't be fooled into thinking that all Egyptian girls are honorable. Some of them are badly brought up and decadent, and they end up doing some shocking things!"

"And what more do they do?"

I raised my head perplexed, "I don't know. Isn't that enough?"

"You're right. It is enough."

2

HE SIGHED, relieved and comfortable in the apartment he had rented in the Zamalek quarter, Cairo's upper-class residential district. It had been a difficult week, but it was over, and his life in Egypt could finally start!

Tomorrow he would start work. He would contact the leasing company that was handling the two apartments that he had bought in London to rent out, with a mortgage underwritten by his employer. One day he would sell them; it would be one of his great deals. He had been endowed with a sharp mind that attracted money like a magnet. How beautiful money is; it can make one a prince or even a king. As long as one has money, one does not need a magic wand or a magic lamp like that of Aladdin, nor does one need to rely on nepotism.

Ashraf was lucky. He had money and he had looks. Of course, he had not been able to work out much over the past few days. He had not been going to the gym to lift weights, but he would get back into it. His aunt's food may have packed on a few pounds, but he would soon start running along the Nile. He loved to work hard and to play hard.

He smiled at himself as he eyed his jeans. Levi's was sure to have a branch in Egypt. He loved the look of white shirts and jeans, especially Levi's, but he figured that it was time to go to the gym.

Tomorrow he would contact Lubna Thaabit. He had not forgotten her, despite his busy schedule.

Who was she, really?

It had not taken Ashraf long to join what he called the "semicultural, semipolitical group" that Lubna hung out with, which was composed of four journalists, including Lubna. They met daily after work in a café, where they would occasionally fight and argue and fail, in most cases, to agree on anything.

What they distinctly shared, in Ashraf's eyes, were anger, ambition, and a frustrated energy, or maybe a love of Egypt. He was not sure, for he had never felt angry on account of a public cause or issue. When he had discussions with others, he preferred either to persuade them or otherwise to bring the discussion to an end. But this group debated and argued endlessly. None among them succeeded in convincing the others of anything.

He had no idea what had brought him to Lubna's circle other than his strong desire for her as a woman. He had never been a patient man, nor had he been interested in politics, but he felt that he was fighting an undeclared war against Lubna and her ideas. It did not take him long to discover that she was a communist. That made him want her even more.

Once a member in her circle said, "Democracy is the solution. We need to give the people back the self-confidence that has been usurped from them for thousands of years."

Another added, "We need to stop patronizing people."

With fake calm Lubna said, "Every country has the system that befits it. In Egypt there is a class so rich it's obscene. It must be done away with, and social justice must be established. We have talked a lot about it in the past, but we have never tried to implement it."

"Communism," Ashraf answered, "is impossible in a country that sanctifies religion, whether Islam or Christianity."

"But communism is an ideology that may be applied anywhere at any time. It may also be placed in a religious context and modeled according to society's needs," Lubna said.

"Were we ever for peace with Israel?" someone asked suddenly.

All fell silent.

Then Ali, who had been somewhat quiet, said, "Yes, but now is not the right time. The peace was sudden, like a shotgun wedding. Everyone was angry because the invitations had arrived too late, and so everyone boycotted the wedding."

They roared with laughter, then one of them rejoined, "We needed peace; it is a lot better than war, Lubna."

"Our war is within; what we need is social justice," Lubna said.

Ashraf was becoming fed up with the discussion, and without concealing his boredom he asked, "What exactly is it that you want, Lubna?"

"I want a lot: social justice, equality, and . . ."

"These are just big words that lost their meaning a long time ago," he interrupted, adding, "What are your political plans? What are your objectives? You're just repeating abstract ideas. That's dangerous. All despots and extremists express abstract ideas that they try to implement in a bunch of different ways at the expense of a whole lot of victims."

Ali asked him suddenly, "And what do you think? What does Egypt need now?"

"Money," Ashraf said confidently.

Lubna gave him a wry look.

"Don't you know something called pride? Egypt once had pride and dignity, but now . . ."

"Pride is bought with money. Moreover, the concept of pride in the Arab world is different from that in the West. Nations have no pride. What they have is interests and money," he asserted firmly.

The quarrel went on for hours, during which Ashraf repeatedly looked at his watch. The party finally broke up, all of them going their separate ways, and Ashraf offered to give Lubna a ride back to work.

Ashraf's opinions in the café had alarmed Lubna. In the car she said sharply, "Listen here, Ashraf, if you want us to remain friends . . ."

"No, I do *not* want us to remain friends," he interrupted.

She stared at him, amazed. He smiled and said "You don't like my views? That is unimportant. I don't want you as a friend, Lubna."

"What do you want?" She was curious.

He smiled as he let her out of the car in front of the newspaper's offices.

"You know what I want?" he asked her.

"No, I don't," she replied, astonished.

"Is it possible to see you tomorrow?"

"For the last two weeks you have seen me every day."

"Yes, but I have had my fill of these discussions. Can I see you elsewhere?" He paused before continuing excitedly, as if the idea had just occurred to him, "Why don't you visit me at my place? I know that means something different in Egypt. But I have never lived in Egypt, and it means nothing to me—just a friend, as you say, visiting another friend. What do you think?"

She narrowed her eyes and looked as if she might hit him, but then she said, "Okay. When?"

"Now, if you want," he said, heaving a sigh of relief.

⌒

Lubna curled up on the big sofa in the living room and wrapped her arms around her legs. Against the luxurious bronze-colored sofa she looked short and small. Her broad facial features were prominent. Piercing him with her eyes, she asked "Who are you?"

"I don't know," he said, smiling as he sat on a chair in front of her.

"A feudalist and a capitalist."

"How do you know that?"

"Your clothes; your fridge, which is crammed with expensive cheese; the pistachios that you carry in your suitcase."

"You opened my fridge and my suitcase?" he asked, pleasantly astonished.

"Of course I did. It is also my job to open other people's hearts. You're Ashraf, the capitalist! Now, listen, tell me about Margaret Thatcher, your prime minister. That woman is a peril to communism and to humanity."

"She wants the economy to flourish," Ashraf smiled.

"She intends to make the rich richer and the poor poorer."

"Without the rich, the poor will never have a happy life. Whenever there is a rich man, he can offer a better life for the poor man."

"That's what the Conservative Party of Britain says. As for me, I believe in social justice," Lubna said.

Ashraf was bored by her words and ideas, but it did not diminish his desire for her. "Would you like some tea?" He rose, heading toward the kitchen.

"Coffee," she said as she took out a cigarette. "I want it black and strong. I need it strong when I have to deal with you. So, what is it you want from me, Ashraf? Despite all the differences between us?"

He wanted to say, "I just want you," but he smiled warmly and said nothing.

She followed him to the kitchen and said animatedly, "For instance, privatization is sure to put an end to social justice. This woman is a tyrant. We thought you had democracy in your country, but it is the democracy of the rich and the suppression of the poor. You know her stance regarding the unions. She treats them as if they were flies that have dropped into her soup bowl."

"You seem to know a lot about British politics," he said, smiling, "but why do you always address me as being British?"

"Aren't you English?" She sighed as she took the cup from him, adding more ground coffee to the cup. "I don't want to think of you as an Egyptian feudalist. If I did, I would hate you, and I don't want to hate you."

He watched her as she stirred and drank her strong coffee as if it were another challenge to be met.

She returned to the bronze-colored sofa, which nearly swallowed her. Taking quick puffs of the cigarette, she gulped her coffee and then said, "I will now have a glass of French white wine. Do you have French wine?"

"I beg your pardon?" His eyes widened.

"You drink alcohol, don't you? What were you doing in that British boarding school other than trying out different types of alcohol and having a taste for all kinds of women?

"Is that what you think I was doing at school?"

"Have you got any wine?"

He nodded.

Her legs were shaking. She grasped the glass with both hands. She gulped the contents in less than a minute.

"You shouldn't drink wine like that," he hastened to comment.

"How then?"

He looked at her briefly, then brought a plate of pistachios and offered her one. He poured wine gently into the glass.

Slowly, enjoying every little sip, Lubna ate some pistachios with the wine.

"The sweet taste will melt into the salted pistachios," he whispered.

She swallowed nervously and rose abruptly. "I have to go home now," she said.

"What for?" he asked innocently. "You know, as we said earlier, that a man and a woman may be together in the same place without committing a sin."

As she ran smiling toward the door she said, "Except that I do not like you to throw me into the sin of luxury, for luxury is a disease without a cure. Good-bye, Ashraf."

"Wait, Lubna," he said earnestly.

He came closer, held her chin, and brought his lips close to hers. His touch was light and tender, and she had never known anything like it. However, he did not kiss her lips but only gave her long kisses on her eyelids, whispering tenderly, "Good-bye."

She left his place in quick, fiery steps.

He felt intoxicated with joy. This woman—how could he describe her? All this culture, charisma, strength, and principles. So different from his British girlfriends. She did not think about women's rights, women's feelings, women's love. She thought about both men and women, about how to change society and everyone around her.

～

Meanwhile, I was busy weaving the story of my love for him in my mischievous, wild, obstinate imagination. I closed the door of my room, which was stuffed with dresses and fabrics. My heartbeats were shaking my whole body. How strong my love for him was! I spent hours listening to the songs of Abdalhaleem. . . . to the sighs, the yearnings, and separation from the beloved one. But it was my imagination, not the sighs, that rocked my feelings. In my mind's eye I could see my cousin as my fiancé. I could see him trying to kiss me for the first time. My body would shudder as I felt him embracing me while I tried to free my body from his arms, but he would only hug me tighter and more strongly. Throughout, he would be frowning and as cruel as a tyrant.

I used to dream, only to hate myself afterward. I hated my dreams and felt ashamed of my imagination. I didn't know why it portrayed for me all these indecencies. I am a model of good manners and reason. I am the one who contains the lapses, and the protector of my sister, Sally, and her adolescence. I am the one who has learned from Mother that virtue is the only weapon of a young woman. It is her wealth and her worth.

One day he would come to ask for my hand in marriage. Everyone, including my mother, shared this feeling. I was looking forward to that day. Today he would have lunch with us. I would cook for him; I would make myself beautiful and wait for him.

I heard Mother screaming, "Get rid of the sitting room dust covers!"

Mother was crazy about the gold-colored living room. The furniture had to be covered when no important people were visiting. I did not notice at the time the meticulous attention to detail that possessed every Egyptian. We are all infatuated with details—even in words, we always read between the lines. But this day Ashraf was coming. We had to strip the faint yellow covers from the gold set—my mother's wedding set and the pride of my father.

I went into the kitchen and started to prepare the salad. I heard Father laughing sarcastically, "Manaal, are you going to make a mess of it today? Do cook something decent, and forget about this messy business of yours. Ashraf is coming from Cairo."

"He likes my cooking," Mother protested.

"No one likes your cooking, Manaal. But what is to be done? Nothing. We have to eat it," he smiled wryly then broke into laughter, which was not shared by my mother.

All that was of no concern to me. The only thing I wanted was to see Ashraf.

⟳

Three months passed, during which Ashraf never ceased attempting to seduce Lubna, to no avail. He felt she was waging a war against him. She seemed to be playing with him, a weird game that he was unable to comprehend. Maybe it was a cold war, like the one between the Soviet Union and the democratic West.

He smiled to himself as he was slicing garlic to add to the pasta. Today he would try once more with Lubna. She would come, and he would try again. He would make dinner for her and set the table. He would give her roses and diamonds if she so wished. They would listen to *Shahrzaad* and *Don Quixote,* and then he would dim the lights so that he would see nothing except the light of her big eyes.

She knocked on the door. He opened it for her as he said sweetly, "My darling!"

She looked at him in a sarcastic and threatening manner. She dashed in, as usual, inspecting everything with her eyes, hands, and nose; the fridge, cupboards, and the food. Then she looked at the dining room, at the pasta with prawns and salmon—she could not imagine where he had gotten all that!

"Have you cooked for me?" she asked as she was taking a seat.

He nodded as he sat opposite her and said, "I've been thinking about you all day. I thought about no one or nothing else: not my work, my family, or even myself."

"Do not say such things. They are all lies. I know," she commented, and added before he could respond, "but you are strange—different, tender, and quiet. You are completely different from my father: I have never seen him cooking dinner for my mother. I have not seen him even talking to Mother. He would always shout at her, and she would apologize. He would sometimes beat her, and she would cry and scream. Poor Father—all that burden: six children, and he was only a messenger boy in the government. What do you expect?"

He did not want to hear Lubna's tragedies or her life story. He had no sympathy for her father, her mother, or for any one but her and her only. She was his target, and he always realized his goals.

She ate in haste, as she always did. Then she sat on the big sofa in the living room. He sat next to her and said nothing. He drew closer and looked into her eyes. He noticed a slight squint in her eyes that was homing in on his.

"I have accepted your offer to come visit you at your place," she whispered softly.

"This is not the first time, Lubna. It means nothing. It does not signify that something will take place between us. True?" he asked.

She nodded and looked away, then she rose as if unsure what to do. She turned, as she often did, and looked around, with her feet moving restlessly, as usual.

"Let's have tea—what do you say? I'll make it," she said eagerly.

She rushed into the kitchen, and started making the tea. He sat on the sofa, lay back, and closed his eyes.

"You are an arrogant feudalist, Ashraf. You have come from an arrogant, greedy, capitalist country," she yelled from the kitchen.

He just smiled, whispering, "You are crazy."

"What did you just say?" she called.

"Nothing. I was saying I do not understand why you believe in communism. A communist system, I believe, is no different from a capitalist one. The privileged strata are the only difference. Every society has privileged strata. Right now in Egypt it is the stratum of businessmen; in Britain it is the stratum of business and the landed gentry. Rather than begrudging this class, Lubna, you should seek to join it. I can help you. Just close your eyes, and when you open them widely you can find yourself in another social stratum."

She shouted back, "I am not one of those privileged thieves, Ashraf. I am not a call girl, and I want nothing from you," she stated angrily.

He said nothing. She brought the tea and sat at the edge of the sofa and said in a bitter tone, with her eyes meeting his, "The rich are full of guilt."

Touching the end of her coarse hair he said tenderly, "And what is wrong with that? So the rich are full of guilt. But they enjoy everything."

"I am beginning to hate you," she said, holding her cup nervously.

"You will not do that ever, Lubna Thaabit, the communist reporter," he whispered as he drew closer to her and sat up. He kissed her cheek tenderly and whispered, "Never!"

"You have come to exploit your people, Ashraf! How different are you from the lady prime minister of Britain? You are exploiting the poor of your country. You sell them pistachios and buy their wheat. No one lives on pistachios, Ashraf," she protested.

He started playing with her hair and said in that warm voice she was becoming addicted to, "Pistachios are delicious, like you: crunchy, small, and salty!"

She said nothing, and both were silent as he stroked her hair. Then she suddenly asked, "Do you want me?"

He looked surprised, then said confidently, "Of course I want you. You are the most beautiful woman I have ever laid eyes on."

"Liar!"

"Believe me, Lubna, I never lie . . . ever."

"But you have come from the country of hypocrisy and occupation."

"I am an Egyptian, exactly like you."

"But you are a member of the British Conservative Party."

He rose and said in a serious tone, "I will be a communist, from now on! From this very moment. What can I to do to prove my goodwill? I will ask the building super to move into my place with me!"

"You're mocking me, Ashraf. Do you know what poverty is? You don't work every day to raise your brother and help your mother. You know nothing except hoarding money and sleeping with women. A hypocrite and a greedy man—that's what you are. I don't know why I bothered to come here . . . or why I'm talking to you. There is no justice in this world."

Before he uttered a single word, she dashed to the door, opened it, and shot out. "Go to hell, Lubna!" he said to himself.

He'd had enough of Lubna, with her unpredictability and attacks. He just wanted to forget about her for a while, starting right then. He wasn't used to having all this longing for a woman. He didn't like sleepless nights, nor did he enjoy being sad. He had no idea what Lubna wanted, exactly. If only she would tell him what she wanted, he would do it immediately, if he could.

Furious, he walked into his bedroom.

To hell with Lubna and to hell with poverty! Why should he care if the whole population were paupers? He was not responsible for their poverty.

He left his bedroom and dropped on the sofa once more. He had never met a woman like her. He had never felt such frustration, and he had never hated communism so much before.

He heard a knock on the door. He dragged himself to his feet, figuring it was the building super. He opened the door and was immediately startled and overjoyed. He was tongue-tied as he looked at her. His arm was blocking the door as if he were preventing crowds from entering.

"Lubna! You didn't leave!" He rested his arm on the door, perplexed.

"May I come in?" she asked

"My home and my heart are yours!" he laughed as he removed his hand.

She came close to him, grasped his arm desperately, as if arresting him, and whispered with desire, "I love you, Ashraf."

◠

He could not understand women. He had thought she was free from him. He had thought that she was in love with conflict and liberty. But all that was in the past. She had surrendered to him and fallen like a leaf in autumn. She just gave herself to him. She closed her eyes and did not pick a single fight. She asked for nothing. She just gave in. He had never felt such desire for any woman before. Her surrender shook him. It drove him to the limit of passion.

She rested her head on his chest as he stretched his legs out on the sofa and said in despair, "I have to leave now, Ashraf."

"Can't you wait till morning?" he whispered as he stroked her forehead.

She rose abruptly, pacing here and there, restless as usual. "I can't do that. Don't forget that we're in Egypt."

"I know."

She sat and suddenly asked, "Why have you not asked me?"

"About what?"

"The first man in my life?"

"I am not interested in knowing that."

"He was a colleague, a journalist, like me," she said as she lit a cigarette.

"I don't want to know." He was faking indifference.

"Did you think I would turn out to be a virgin?"

In fact, Ashraf did not know whether or not she was. "That is of no interest to me, Lubna," he said smiling.

"But you want to know. You expected me to be a virgin. As an Egyptian girl, you expected that I was either a virgin or a tart."

"We are not going to fight now, Lubna," he said softly.

"I am not a tart, Ashraf. Have I asked you for anything? If I were, I would have asked for something in return, anything!" she said, as if pleading hopelessly before a judge.

"Lubna . . ."

"I am not a loose girl," she interrupted hysterically. "I love you, I . . ."

"Lubna, listen to me," he interrupted.

"I submitted to you because I love you—do you understand? There are tarts, but there are girls who have liberated themselves from . . ."

"Lubna!" he shouted, turning her face toward him. "Listen to me. I have not been raised in Egypt. I do not think you are loose, and I don't care about your past. I care only about your present. I don't think that women surrender to men, though I felt like you submitted to me. But I hope that in the future you do not offer yourself as a gift to me, but that both of us should do the giving. Do you understand?"

She shook her head and asked, "Are you going to ask me why he deserted me?"

"Because he is a fool," he said nervously.

"No, he had to leave me."

"He died?"

"He was detained. He was an Iraqi journalist."

"You like trouble, don't you? Is he still alive?" He smiled warmly.

"I saw him a year ago. He was a different man. I didn't know him anymore."

"Had he been tortured?"

"I don't know. Except he was different. He spent three years away from me. I knew nothing about him. I never expected to see him again. When he arrived I had already convinced myself that he was dead."

Then suddenly, she whispered in panic, "Ashraf . . ."

"Capitalists do not go to prison except perhaps in the Soviet Union. We are in Egypt. Don't worry about me. Do you love him?"

"It is you I love."

"You don't still love him even a little bit?"

"I love only you, but you frighten me: I despise your wealth and hate pistachios. Now take me to my home in the Imbaba quarter. Do you know where that is?" she asked as she headed for the door.

"No," he smiled as he walked by her side, "but it is a great place if it has produced fighters of your caliber."

～

I began spending a long time in my room, lying on my bed dreaming. When Mother called for me, interrupting my beautiful dream, I was always on the verge of tears.

Once more, I would dream of him being my husband. I would dream of the wedding night as he kissed me for the first time . . . I being the shy one and he reassuring me . . . but I would not be reassured; I would resist him, so he would pounce on me with vigor and mercilessness and false tenderness.

I would fight him back, but he would defeat me. I dreamed of his yearning and desire, of his touching me tenderly and firmly, thus protecting and nourishing me.

There was one particular dream that I liked most: he would have a quarrel with me because he was jealous of another man. He would order me not to leave the house and to stop taking classes, so I would react sharply. He would then twist my wrist until I agreed, but I would feel sad about it. Then he would melt me in his arms and vanquish me once more. He would embrace me firmly and overwhelm me completely until I became one with him, living in him and totally dependent on him. He would not be able to survive for a moment without me.

I wanted him cruel and strong. I never liked tender men. I wanted him violent and high-strung. I wanted him jealous and in control of me, but infatuated with me. Let him overcome me with vigor and violence. I would submit to him reluctantly; then I would submit wholeheartedly.

I waited for his weekly and sometimes monthly visits. I filled up with his presence, and then I would go back to my dreams once more. In those days I dreamed a lot. Sometimes I pretended to be asleep and would lose myself in my daydreams. I felt that some day he would come. He would confess his love. Naturally, he would not choose a prostitute like Lubna as a wife. When the man wanted to get married, he would marry a girl like me. I would do my makeup and wait.

I imagined his hand stroking my arm, and fire broke out inside my whole body, a fire I have never thought was there inside me, accompanied by a frightful and delicious yearning.

When he arrived he was not alone. He came today accompanied by Lubna Thaabit. It didn't matter. I could not be made to feel jealous of a prostitute. My mother said that a man had certain needs that were understood by prostitutes only. But when a man made up his mind to marry, he would pick a good, innocent girl from a respectable family and forget all about prostitutes. I did not feel jealous of Lubna; she was nothing. In fact, I wanted to see her so that I would not end up looking as cheap and as vulgar as she was: she was like a man disguised as a woman.

I looked at Lubna as she sat beside my sweetheart. I inspected her. My mother smiled, even laughed, as she welcomed Lubna more warmly than necessary. "And you, what do you write about?"

"About people and their usurped rights."

My mother nodded as if she understood everything. She asked no more questions. After lunch Lubna lit a cigarette and relaxed in the gold-colored living room. May she never rise from her seat ever, the degenerate!

Ashraf looked happy. Why was he looking happy?

Our eyes, Lubna's and mine, met. She stretched her hand out and held Ashraf by the arm as if he were part of the property she had owned before the Suez Canal was nationalized and her family had to move to a working-class quarter of Cairo.

It didn't matter. None of it mattered. He was still young. When he matured, he would find me waiting. But when he interlaced his fingers with Lubna's, I shivered despite myself, and I escaped to my room. I closed my eyes as I sat on my bed and imagined myself as Lubna. I envied her: if only I had her forwardness; if only I could one day hold his hand like that.

It was only occasionally that I wished I were Lubna. But these were devilish dreams. It was a test I had to pass. I was not Lubna. Lubna would not win the game. Good would prevail in the end.

∾

When Lubna returned with Ashraf to his house she seemed gloomy. "That girl loves you," she said as she drank her beer and smoked her cigarettes. "Do you know that?"

"Are you jealous of her, darling?" he said as he came closer with that irresistible smile.

"Of course not. But she loves you. I want you to watch out. Naïve girls can be a real danger for men," she said sternly.

"What can she do?" he whispered as he embraced her.

"You knew she's in love with you?" she asked sharply.

"Of course I knew."

She moved away from him and said, staring at him, "What kind of game are you playing?"

"I am not playing any game," he said innocently.

"Indeed you are. Why do you want to torture her?"

He moved away from her and said, sounding puzzled, "What is this nonsense?"

"What do you want from her? I know you."

He pondered briefly, then said, "I may be trying to shatter her rigidity, her obsolete traditions."

"You mean her beliefs? You think her beliefs are obsolete traditions?"

He nodded.

"And how do you intend to do that? By seducing her?"

He looked as furious as if she had asked him to eat snails with Western cheese and red onions. "Your opinion of me is exceedingly bad. I don't seduce girls, especially if I don't like them. I just wish her to experience the pain, let go of her rigidity, and become aware of what is happening around her. I don't like ignorance, stagnation, and beliefs that are as ancient as the era of pharaohs."

"What do you want her to do, have an affair? Lose her virginity? In our society?"

"Perhaps, maybe . . . she has to live as she desires, not as society wants her to live. She must not respect her brother more than she respects her sister. She has to be like you, Lubna."

"A communist?"

"To have opinions of her own, any opinions. I have never seen a woman like you, either in Britain or in Egypt. Let's forget about Wafaa. You, Lubna . . . ," he paused as he came closer to her.

"I am what?"

"You are the life that I have never lived nor known."

After he'd made love to her, he stretched his legs out on the big bed, closed his eyes, and whispered as if talking to himself. "Lubna."

She tore herself away from his side, saying, "I'm hungry. Let's eat something. I'll cook for you."

"I'll cook for you," he said calmly with his eyes closed. "You stay here, darling. Don't move."

〜

He rose. She looked at him with her heart throbbing because of his tenderness, which she had never known from any man. She loved him passionately, and she did not know how to get rid of this love. She sighed and closed her eyes again. For a brief moment she forgot where she was and what her mission in life was. She forgot what time it was. She forgot all about Damanhour and about Wafaa. What did she want from him? What did this stupid girl expect?

If he married Wafaa, she would kill him. If he married someone else, she would kill him as well. How strong her desire was to kill him!

∽

He came back with a tray stuffed with imported cheese, Western-type bread, and caviar. She sighed once more and said, "I thought you were going to cook for me."

"I didn't want to waste time in cooking. We have little time left. I want to be by your side, yours alone! I want you to stay here forever. I wish that we could forget about the whole world, the Imbaba quarter, politics, your brother, your mother, my maternal aunt, any work, and . . ."

"Wafaa," she interrupted threateningly.

"I do not remember her at all." He smiled mockingly.

"Do you hate her?"

Bored, he rested his head on his pillow and said, "We talked about that earlier."

"Let's talk about it again! Tell me first about yourself, pistachio seller," she dared him.

He closed his eyes and said, as if to himself, "An introverted, spoiled child torn between mother and father."

"Your parents aren't on good terms with each other?"

"On very bad terms," he said indifferently.

"Does your mother hate your father?"

"Exceedingly so," he said mechanically. He paused briefly and added, as if he suddenly remembered something important, "Wafaa sometimes reminds me of my mother!"

"That's why you hate her."

"I may pity her, sometimes. I hate Wafaa and love my mother passionately."

"And whom do you pity?"

"My mother, of course. She lived imprisoned by Umm Kulthoum's songs. She has not broken free from her chains, whereas Father prides himself on his British passport. He meets lords and boasts about civilization and progress, while she listens to songs and curses the occupying forces, moral decomposition, and licentiousness." He frowned as he thought about his mother and the narrow life she led in Great Britain. She never coped, nor did she ask for divorce. She lacked imagination. Yes—the problem with Wafaa and with his mother was that for both of them, life was devoid of imagination.

∼

That was what Ashraf thought. He knew nothing about my wild imagination.

∼

He looked at Lubna's big eyes, at the slight squint with which he was familiar. She looked like a wild cat, set to attack, skinny and with eyes that stared at everything and nothing. He smiled and held her hand. He grasped it between his hands and whispered; "Lubna, you are the most splendid woman I have ever laid eyes on. If only you would shut up and stop repeating all this nonsense."

She wanted to scream, to sever her relationship with him. But his hand covered her mouth. No man had ever treated her that way.

Muhannad, the Iraqi journalist, had been tender with her, but not that tender. His touch was hurried and practical; he was a revolutionary with little time for love. As for Ashraf, love was a game at which he excelled. He made her anxious and provoked her weakness and her fury.

She rose abruptly from bed, dressed, and held her purse as he was eyeing her with his mocking smile. "I have to go. I don't want to listen to your provocations," she protested with her usual anger.

But he said nothing.

She opened the door wide. Stretching out on the bed, he said, "Goodbye, Lubna." She didn't respond, but her steps were rather hesitant. He shouted across the bedroom, "See you tomorrow?" It was posed as a question, but he got the answer he expected.

"Yes," she said mechanically. She closed the door behind her and raced down the stairs, her heart pounding and her mind racing.

∼

His love for her was like the Olympic torch, hot and burning. I think she loved him, too. He believed that she loved him, if prostitutes have hearts. In old films they did. Prostitutes were forced to earn money that way. But

Lubna was a special type of prostitute. Not to worry! She might be in love with him. I don't want to talk about this now . . . Let's talk about something else.

∾

My sister had become unbearable. I began to fear for her unknown future. She could end up like Lubna. I should have told our parents, although I might have had to wait a little before informing Father. I watched her. She was talking to a man—again! I told Kareem that I had my doubts about Sally and that, as the man of the house, he had to do something about it. Kareem was sixteen. Like a rooster, he preened his feathers and went after her. He interrogated her, and she broke down and confessed. My brother pulled her hair and threatened her. She looked at me with hatred in her eyes but said nothing. As for Mother, she said angrily, "Sally, wise up before we tell your father. I don't want you near this telephone again." She added, "Kareem, my darling, come here. It's time to eat."

On the same day my mother and I had been extraordinarily proud because Kareem had used the phone to talk to his girlfriend. There was a great difference between men and women.

∾

Ashraf's affair with Lubna had not been a continuous ecstasy, for Lubna was high-strung and crazy, and she was energetic as well, as energetic and active as a deer caught in headlights. Her feelings toward him fluctuated between possessiveness and hatred, accompanied by jealousy. She started paying surprise visits to him at the bank, and woe unto him if she found him talking to another woman! She would grow extremely agitated; she would scream at him in the apartment and smash dishes to pieces. He would try to calm her, and she would end up dropping her head to his chest while threatening and abusing him. Her situation was extremely humiliating. Yes, she had known it all along, certainly. She had not asked for marriage, nor had he offered to marry her, but he had better watch out if he ever tried to buy her. He once bought her a present, a gold ring. She hit the roof, once more, and cried her eyes out. "You think I'm a call girl? You think you can buy me with your money?" she screamed in his face.

He took her to a five-star hotel for dinner. Then he suggested that they could stay there for the night. She insisted once more that she hated money and loathed wealthy people, including himself. She vanished for days and days. He had known all along that she would return after a while to throw herself against his chest and give herself to him.

～

In that, Lubna was not much different from other women. They were all from the same rib. She knew that when she first went to his place that she, in effect, had offered herself to him, even if she didn't submit her body to him in that instance, but only afterwards, if you know what I mean.

She must have felt severe insecurity and perhaps a twinge of guilt. I didn't know for sure. She may have been living with him in reality, not in a dream.

How I hated her!

It was nothing to worry about. In fact, I knew Ashraf and knew about his problem with Lubna. It was an intellectual problem, I figured. Ashraf loved money and the easy life. He loved to spend time in the hot tub and at the gym. He loved to eat caviar in expensive restaurants, French pastries, and Swiss chocolate. He didn't know the Imbaba quarter. He tried to spend most of his time in Zamalek or Muhandiseen, either working, gambling, or drinking champagne. He wanted to spoil and pamper her. He wanted to make her his princess. She refused proudly, and he loved her for that. He never tried to enter the Imbaba quarter, just as she hated to enter Zamalek. Neither would become part of the other's world.

3

HE HELD THE REMOTE CONTROL and sent the toy car fast in the direction of the kitchen. Then he changed its direction—the living room, the hall, and then the kitchen again. The car would go around the table, then into the hall and the kitchen once more, as his thumb pressed the button eagerly.

He was used to solitude and had become addicted to toy cars. He had been familiar with solitude since he was a shy, introverted child. He had been addicted to playing with toy cars since puberty. He was a different child, an Egyptian attending British schools, and he did not succeed in making friends among the boys. However, he was better at winning girlfriends. Playing with toy cars and women used to be his real joy. But he was impatient; he would quickly get fed up with women. He never got impatient with toy cars.

When he heard his mother screaming and crying, he would withdraw into himself inside his room instead of hugging her. He would play with his cars, tanks, and planes. He would wage war on everyone. He always won.

His fingers were pushing the button wildly when he heard the telephone ringing.

He rested the set against his shoulder as he used the remote control to move his car all over the place. The minute his mother's voice reached him, he said tenderly, "Mother, how are you, dear?"

"Ashraf, what are you doing with this loose girl I'm hearing about?" she inquired anxiously.

"I'm working, Mother, writing a report about a new bank client," he said earnestly, as he was chasing the toy car with his eyes and pushing the button.

"Ashraf, where have you gone?"

"Just reading some papers."

"Look after yourself."

She hung up. He wanted to enjoy his solitude. He took another car out of the cupboard. He opened the box eagerly. He was soon playing with two cars, pushing the buttons feverishly.

His phone rang again. He felt as disappointed as a groom whose bride had been abducted on their wedding day. "Yes?" he said tersely.

"What are you doing?" Lubna rejoined sharply.

"I'm working," he said impatiently.

"I miss you," she whispered.

He said nothing. His eyes were chasing the cars.

"Who is there with you, Ashraf?" she said angrily.

He sighed and said impatiently, "Again, Lubna?"

"Who is there with you?" she shouted.

He looked at the time. It was two o'clock in the morning.

"Come and see for yourself," he said, defiant but eager.

"Liar!" she screamed. "You know I can't come."

Faking surprise, he rejoined, "Why? You are equal to a hundred men!"

"Ashraf . . ."

"Good night," he interrupted her sharply. He put the receiver down and breathed heavily, irritated.

As for her, she put on her clothes and looked around briefly. She knew that her mother was asleep and her brother would not come home then. She left in the raw fury that always fueled her. She flagged down a taxi and headed for Ashraf's place.

The fire inside her was heating her arms all the way down to her hands. She didn't know whether this was the fire of her longing for him—or was it the fire of jealousy, or the flames of her guilt feelings, or the heat of her anger?

No—she did know. Of course she did. "My heart is moved only by anger," she thought. Anger is king, and all the other emotions are nothing but his foot soldiers.

She knocked on the door. There was no answer.

She knocked again, shouting, "Open up, Ashraf, you traitor. I will kill you today, now! I will do it!"

He opened the door and looked puzzled. "Are you off your rocker? My God!"

She swept into the apartment, searching every room like a security guard.

"These sudden visits belong to the socialist regime that you admire. Or is it a mere rehearsal for your new role in the intelligence service?" he whispered sarcastically.

Still furious, she finished her inspection. Eyeing him fiercely, she demanded, "Stop mocking me!"

"Wait a minute!" he said impatiently. "This doesn't make any sense. First you accuse me of being disloyal and treacherous, you scream at me, and then you search my place! Lubna, I fear for Egypt from the likes of you! Where is the justice you hope for?"

She looked around her at the toy cars, the expensive fountain pens, and the elegant desk, and she was bitter. "You love whatever is expensive, trivial and without value."

"Let me take you home, darling," he interrupted her, bored.

She wanted to tear him to pieces first. She wanted to taste pistachios (which she feared and loved at the same time). She collapsed on the chair, desperate and furious. "I will stay, but only an hour!"

He smiled, feeling victorious as usual.

∾

Do you remember the love of youth (not adolescence, for I was not an adolescent, though I loved him as one)? My heart would keep pounding, and my legs would be shaking because he would be there in a week's time. When I saw him I would be speechless. I would blink repeatedly.

That day he was due to arrive on his own, not accompanied by that whore. Mother was stuffing vegetables, which she knew Ashraf liked. Today I would speak to him. I would ask him not to link his future to that woman. His mother had phoned me the day before. She was crying. She'd thought he would return to Egypt to marry someone who would cater to him, not someone who would destroy his honor. She had feared that he would marry a girl from the West, and here he was falling in love with an infidel whore from Egypt.

"He doesn't love her," I told my mother firmly.

"I don't know. He shouldn't trust the likes of her. She may trap him with a baby or something."

In fear I fell silent. When he knocked I hastened to open the door. I gazed at him as he smiled proudly. What was it that dazzled me? His jeans, his white shirt? His pointed face? His big eyes? His intelligence and his arm? I used to love his left arm, his silver watch, and his soft voice. I had no idea whether I also loved the glitter of the West and its culture, or his ambition, money, and everything.

He came in and sat with Father. I could not get control of myself. I was silent behind the door when I heard him say, "Uncle, I don't like the way you invest your money."

"We have two apartments rather than one. We have two stores, not just one," my father rejoined proudly.

"Yes. You have an empty house that takes money, not makes it. A house is not a secure investment. The security is to make your money work all the time. Stagnation is no good."

"What does that mean? Does it mean I should rent out the apartment? I am keeping it for Kareem when he gets married."

"Then rent it out until Kareem gets married. You can't keep waiting for his marriage."

Mother entered and said eagerly, "Enough talk. Come and eat. Ashraf, I would like to speak with you, darling."

He heaved a deep sigh and rose, expecting what she would say.

"Do not make your mother angry, son. This girl is no good."

"No good for what?" he asked, eyeing her, astonished.

"No good for you to marry."

He smiled once more and said nothing, as if he had not heard a single word she'd said.

As for me, I was looking forward to telling him my views about Lubna and my hatred of her. Mother left us together in the family room after lunch.

I was provoking him. This gelatinous, snail-like brain of mine provoked him.

"You dislike Lubna. You think she's cheap," he said, sipping his tea.

His remarks took me by surprise. My lack of sharpness manifested itself, as usual. My eyes started their endless blinking.

He smiled mockingly and said, "Wafaa, I'm like your older brother. Tell me what you think about Lubna. Why do you hate her so much?"

I looked away and mumbled as if talking to myself, "She gave herself to you free of charge, for nothing."

I had taken him by surprise again. Stunned, he asked, "Should she have taken a price for that?"

Avoiding his eyes again, I said, "Yes. The price was your life. Your commitment to her, for her. However, she gave herself to you for nothing. She's not cheap. She's more like free of charge."

"Wafaa, I have spent my youth in another country. My views are different from yours."

"But she is Egyptian, exactly like myself," I said, staring severely at him.

"She has granted me nothing. She gives and she takes. Women do not give men anything for nothing."

I was puzzled. I didn't know what to say.

He continued eagerly, "In our relationship we're equals."

"You're not equals," I snapped. "Women are different from men. Man does not carry his shame with him. He doesn't give birth. He doesn't suffer. But women are in a different position. What does a woman gain from a degenerate relationship like this one?"

"What does she gain? She loves me as I love her. She gains what I gain," he smiled, surprised.

I shook my head energetically as I rose. "No. You're a man. You can marry another woman afterward. You can forget her. You're a man. She means nothing to you. If she were a woman with a speck of pride, she would have preserved herself. She . . ."

"That's enough, Wafaa. We are in complete disagreement," he interrupted me, sounding bored.

But I rejoined hesitantly, "And another thing. My aunt Aliyya says alcohol burns its user. I fear for you, Ashraf. I am afraid of the demons who will burn you alive."

He was silent. I didn't know if he was irritated or just puzzled.

"Wafaa, you always surprise me. You repeat like a parrot what your aunt says. Who is she? And what is she to me? Do you really believe your words are going to affect me?" he said quietly.

I hastened to rejoin, "Ashraf, my aunt Aliyya is pious and knows everything."

He heaved a deep sigh and asked in a tight voice, "What about you? Don't you know anything at all? What do you know exactly?"

My temperature started rising as I replied, "But I have to listen to those who know. She's knowledgeable. She knows everything. You also know that alcohol isn't permitted in Islam."

"Do you believe what you're saying? All you talk about is afterlife torture, demons, and graphic details about pain for sinners. Do you have anything bigger to think about? You're interested in the small details, but who are you? What relationship do you have with God?" He sounded extremely irritated, for the first time ever.

I repeated, "You know that alcohol is not permitted in Islam."

"Yes, I know that. But when I stop drinking, it won't be because I'm afraid but because I am convinced. Do you understand? The difference between you and me is that you are afraid of everything. You perform your religious rites because you're afraid. Fear is disgusting."

I didn't utter a word. He was cruel to me. He was really cruel.

But wasn't cruelty what I was after? His cruelty was here in my grasp. He was cruel.

I didn't like his cruelty, but I wasn't angry with him. I left the room quietly. His eyes were gleaming with fury.

～

A few seconds later Sally entered the room with a grim face. She looked at Ashraf hopefully.

"What's wrong?" He smiled affectionately

"Wafaa told Kareem, who beat me and grounded me. I haven't seen Ahmed for a whole week. Help me, Ashraf. Ahmed will hate me. He may leave me. If he does, I'll leave home. I will," she said, sobbing.

"I'll talk to Kareem," he said, patting her shoulder tenderly.

"Speak with Wafaa. She's behind everything. Marry her, Ashraf. Please do it so she'll get off my back."

He rose, laughing, and said, "I'll talk to her, Sally."

～

What happened afterward was my story, the whole of my tragedy, with delusion and reality rolled into one. Sometimes short moments can shape our lives forever, although others might see such moments as insignificant.

Ashraf entered the kitchen and said quietly, "Wafaa."

I looked shyly at him and said, "Yes, Ashraf."

"May I speak to you?"

"Of course, Ashraf." I looked at him. My heart sank.

I headed for the family room, but he said firmly, "In your room."

I froze in panic and happiness and headed for my room. I opened the door and said, bewildered, "Sorry, Ashraf. My room is a mess. I'm usually a tidy person. By God, I clean my room every day, but today I was helping Mother in the kitchen and . . ."

He was not listening. He looked around. I remembered the Egyptian film *The Bride's Mother*, where the groom, played by Yousif Shaaban, entered the room of his bride-to-be, played by Sameerah Ahmed, who then said proudly, "You are the first man to enter my room."

The words echoed in my mind, so I blurted them out, "You are the first man to enter my room."

"And Kareem and your father, are they not men? Haven't they ever entered this room?" He laughed as he stood there.

"I mean a man . . . a man," I said, confused.

He shook his head sarcastically and repeated, "Yes. A man." He looked around my room once more. He looked at the textbooks scattered over the bed and the desk and on the floor and smiled.

I felt embarrassed again and said, "I'm really sorry, Ashraf, the room is not . . ."

He interrupted me as he sat on the bed. He was looking directly into my eyes when he said, "It doesn't matter, Wafaa. I have come here to talk to you about an important matter." He stretched out on the bed, resting his head against his folded hands. He saw shyness spreading all over my face as I broke into a sweat.

"Wafaa! What is wrong with you?"

I leaned against the door, interlacing my fingers, and said somewhat nervously, "I know. You want to talk to me about Sally. Is that it?"

Our eyes met, as he said, "Sit down, Wafaa."

I sat at my desk, holding fast to a book, nervously, as if I feared losing it.

He rested his leg on the bed, as if that were his natural space. I have never imagined that the day would come when Ashraf would stretch out on my bed, my very bed. I couldn't stop fantasizing; I would soon be in his arms in my bed. Vicious fantasies planted in my mind by demons!

"You can't punish your sister just for being in love."

"I'm not punishing her because she's in love. I fear for her. She is young and may be exploited by that man. Besides, there are limits and boundaries that we must . . ."

"You treat her like she's an idiot. Let her have the freedom to choose. She is responsible for her own acts. How come you respect your brother, who is five years your junior, and don't respect your sister?" he interrupted me, sitting up.

"My brother is a man. He loses nothing. But my sister stands to lose everything," I said automatically.

"Lose everything! Your sister? Wafaa, she loves this man and wants to marry him."

Pressing the book more firmly to my chest, I heard myself saying, "I don't want her to become like that loose girl of yours. I don't want her to end up being a degenerate."

He looked like he felt a wild urge to spit in my face and scream, "You are the stupidest woman I have ever laid eyes on!"

But he didn't say that. He heaved a deep sigh and said, "Cousin, Lubna is not a loose girl."

I turned my face away so that he would not see the hurt in my eyes and said nothing. I just smiled sarcastically. He saw my smile. He rose and went for the door, probably thinking how stupid and naïve I was, with my snail-like brain. You could either crush a snail with your foot or leave it to crawl slowly inside its narrow shell.

He stopped suddenly and looked at my back as I sat on the chair, hugging that book to my chest.

He touched my shoulder tenderly . . . and so I sighed deeply, in panic, and turned to face him. I looked at him with a mixture of yearning, fear, and confusion.

This comforted him. He had seen the love in my eyes since the beginning. Now he saw it more clearly. He moved his hand away from my shoulder and turned his hands slowly toward my face. He placed his fingers on my cheek. I pushed his hand away reluctantly, and he whispered my name as he moved nearer.

I felt his breath on my cheek, so I swallowed once more, feeling like a frightened animal. I was wet with perspiration. I was speechless. He kicked the door closed and held my hand.

I opened my mouth to speak, but he held my face again and said, "Wafaa, don't be afraid."

I was shaken like never before. Then I was frozen. I closed my eyes, and every bit of me longed for him. It was like he had set fire to my heart. I never realized that my heart was that flammable. His hands covered my cheeks, and I felt like I was in a different world. He whispered again as the back of his hand caressed my cheeks slowly and expertly, "Love is beautiful, Wafaa. Do not deprive your sister of it. It's unfair, Wafaa, unfair."

I said nothing. Everything was happening all at once. I didn't know what to do. I would stop him. Yes, I would. He began stroking my cheeks, and a shameful longing broke out inside me. His fingers then stroked my neck, then my arm, and I shuddered, not fully realizing what was happening.

He smiled victoriously, opened the door, and left quietly without uttering a word.

〜

Outside, he heaved a deep sigh. He had no tolerance for this. He didn't know why he'd been that cruel. He was sometimes in the habit of attacking the points of weakness of his adversaries. This time he felt no guilt because these principles provoked and saddened him.

〜

I threw my body on my bed and smiled to myself. I entered my private world; the fire he lit would not leave me. What had he done? He had touched my cheeks, my neck, and my arms. Hadn't he? Hadn't he? I was certain that he had, and I am still certain. The truth was much more beautiful than my dreams

I felt his warm hand as a puppy would feel its mother approaching from a distance. That day I decided that Ashraf was to be the father of my children, my husband, and my sweetheart. He didn't know, as yet, about this decision of mine. But he would soon know it, very soon indeed. In fact, a man would not touch a woman that way unless he was in love with her. I was sure.

∼

It seemed that good fortune smiled on me at long last. Within a week, my mother decided that we had to visit our aunt in Cairo for the wedding of her daughter, Abla. As my aunt's house was small, and my mother couldn't stand her anyway, she decided we would all stay at Ashraf's. Father made no objection. The real reason was Mother's curiosity about Ashraf's Zamalek apartment, the apartment she believed would soon be her daughter's. She had to invite Ashraf to the wedding and to insist and persist until he accepted the invitation, for when he had a taste of weddings he would certainly look forward eagerly to his own.

My heart pounded all the way to Cairo. I spent the time dreaming again. No sooner had we arrived than I felt my whole body trembling, like never before. Our eyes met. He smiled at me, then kissed Mother. We walked into his gorgeous apartment.

Mom drew breath through her teeth as she eyed the large window overlooking the river, the modern living room, the black leather-bound books, the huge table, and the small window connecting the kitchen with the dining room. And it was there that Mother saw a bottle of wine. She pursed her lips and frowned in disappointment.

"What would you like to drink, Aunt?"

Ashraf sounded like he had understood what she was thinking and wanted to mock and tease her.

Mom rose and said, as she poked my side, "We'll make ourselves at home, my darling. Wafaa and Sally will get up and get some juice or something for their brother and father."

I rose shyly and stood, puzzled.

Ashraf smiled, saying, "I have cooked for you today, Aunt. Of course, my food isn't like yours. It's just pasta and chicken." He looked at me and said tenderly, "Wafaa, come with me."

Had he said it? Really?

He had said, "Come with me, Wafaa."

I closed my eyes for a couple of seconds and then headed for the kitchen with my eyes wide open, stunned. He had cooked! He had washed dishes. Him. A man with all that tenderness and affection. However, after marriage, I wouldn't want him to cook. All I would want was for him to love me. I wanted to be his. I wanted to give myself to him as a gift and to enjoy the mere fact of being with him. I closed my eyes so that he wouldn't see in them my desire and longing. Once more I would see him tearing off my clothes mercilessly before dissolving me inside himself.

His hands stretched out with the dishes. "Here you are, Wafaa."

I opened my eyes in panic. I looked at him. My head was swimming with fantasies—him kissing and kissing me, his grip hurting me. I loved this type of pain. His hands over my body, declaring his full control over me.

"Wafaa."

"I'm sorry," I said, shaken. I stretched my hand to reach the dishes.

As he was handing them over to me, he said suddenly, "A penny for your thoughts?"

Oh, my God. Had he read my mind already, then?

In my head I heard Aunt Aliyya screaming, "Taboo! *Prohibited*, Wafaa. The devil is taking you under his control!"

He smiled and said softly, "I'll carry the plates."

I said apologetically, "It was a long trip from Damanhour to Cairo."

He smiled as he went toward the kitchen door carrying the plates. "Yes, I know."

We sat, all of us, around the table. My mother was saying once more to him, "Get married, darling. Find a girl to cherish and protect you."

He said nothing. So Kareem hastened to say, "I'll marry a foreign girl and leave here."

"What a calamity! Shut up, boy!"

Sally intervened with her usual curiosity, "Did you have a girlfriend in Britain?"

Father look at her with reproach. She fixed her eyes on the floor and said nothing.

When we finished eating, Sally grabbed me by the hand mischievously and said, "Come on. Hurry!"

We walked along the corridor where the guest room, the bathroom, and his bedroom were located.

Sally pushed open the door to his room gently and said, "Come on in. Let's see what's inside. Do you think that girl is living with him?"

"This is terrible, Sally. What if Mother finds out?"

She said, sounding bored, "You're going to tell Mother it's okay and to let us make the tea."

"I will not tell her that," I hastened to say.

She looked at me, surprised, and said as she stepped cautiously into the room, "Come with me."

I entered and could hear my heart pounding. I held fast to my younger sister's hand, and she whispered, "What is it, Wafaa? Why is your hand so cold? Are you robbing a bank? This is your cousin's room."

My eyes were riveted on the bed. My heart ached and I heard his voice in my mind: "I love you, Wafaa. You are mine. You belong to me. You are part of me, and you are mine. Let's forget the past, Wafaa. From this day forward I don't want you to think about anything except me. Wafaa, you are not to go out without my permission. No one except me may see your face, Wafaa."

Sally's voice shook me awake. "Look, a comb, a perfume bottle, and lipstick. I knew it all along. Your cousin does a lot of work in this bed. Have you seen the types of liquor he drinks? Ashraf is sweet, but he is a devil. How I envy him!" She was being mischievous.

"Don't talk like that. It's disgraceful, Sally. I'm going to tell Mother," I said angrily and in despair.

She sprayed perfume over her hand and sniffed it. "It smells good. Do you think he bought it for her?"

I was in a total panic and threw myself on the bed when he suddenly appeared at the door. He looked at Sally with a mixture of mockery and admiration but said nothing.

"Ashraf . . . I was . . . I was just looking for sugar. Do you have some in here?" Sally asked.

"No. There's no sugar here," he said, shaking his head and suppressing his laughter.

Sally put the perfume back and ran in the direction of the kitchen.

"I'll look for it in the bathroom—I mean the kitchen."

I'd risen and started toward the door when he called out, "Wafaa . . ."

I said nothing. I stopped, blind to what was around me.

"I didn't know you were this naughty and sly!" he whispered as he approached me.

"Me?" I said, my hands shaking.

He put his hand on mine and said gently, "Why are you shaking?"

"Ashraf," I whispered, pulling my hand from his.

"Yes," he said confidently.

"You never answered my question."

"I know."

"Does she come to you here?"

He nodded.

"She is a loose girl. She has no family to teach her manners," I said angrily.

"She loves me."

"No. She does not love you. If she loved you, she would have preserved her honor. What torture awaits her on the Day of Judgment," I said with venom.

He just smiled sarcastically as I said in earnest, "Do you know that people like her, when they are in their graves, will receive the most severe punishment and torture? I read it in a book about torture in graves."

He nodded, faking seriousness, as if in agreement with me, and then he said, "Will you be sleeping here, you and Sally? The apartment only has two bedrooms. I think you and Sally will sleep here, and your mother and father will sleep in the second room. Kareem and I will take the living room."

He walked past the bed. He placed his hand on it and slowly started stroking the right-hand side of the bed as he said, "Here. Is this where you will sleep?"

My stomach ached. I didn't know what the problem was. My whole body was in turmoil. I was lusting after him the way a whore would. I hated myself for it.

Our eyes met. I understood nothing. Or maybe I did.

"I sleep here every night," he whispered, smiling sweetly.

"Every night?" I repeated dumbly.

"Every night," he said softly, seductively, as he headed toward the door.

My sole wish and desire was to sleep in his room. But it was not to be. I slept—or, rather, spent a sleepless night—in the guest room. I was deep in thought about his words and his tenderness. He was tender, but I was confused about it. I could not work it out: there was an Ashraf Daawood imprinted on the curvature of my mind and an Ashraf Daawood who lived in the Zamalek quarter.

He smiled to himself. He might even have chuckled. He was playing a game with me, and I didn't know a thing about it. He loved playing games. He was molding me like clay.

I will never forgive him.

∼

Had he known me, he would have loved me. I was sure of that. He needed to know me better. He needed to spend more time with us. Yes, he loved me. He just needed more time.

Tonight was Abla's wedding party. Abla is my aunt Aliyya's daughter. He would fall in love with me there. I wanted to be the most beautiful girl at the reception. I wore a long glittering dress with puffed sleeves.

I heard the drums. The wedding procession began. The bride and groom appeared. I had goose bumps, a quake of longing and yearning. Women's trilling sounds of joy reverberated as the bride smiled. Her eyes were filled with panic. I felt tears welling in my own eyes. I wished to see him there and then. I was so young. I thought: O Lord, make him come. Sorry, God, for all the vile thoughts in my mind. Please, God, I want to see him.

I sat waiting for him. My eyes searched for him everywhere. I sat by Mother's side like a good pupil petrified by the headmistress's ruler. I hate pain and torture. Sally tried to pull me by the hand to dance with her. But I looked at Mother and said to her impatiently, "No, this can't be. It's not allowed."

At long last I saw him. He was wearing a black suit and seemed lost amid the dancing, the noise, and the laughter. He looked a lot younger in his black suit. I closed my eyes and sighed deeply. Then I followed him with my eyes. As he approached, my heart throbbed. I hoped that he would sit beside us even briefly. The music drowned out his voice. He looked elegant, smart, smiling, and confident. But the look of loss never left his eyes. As for my eyes, they were devouring him, hesitantly and in panic.

I willed him to come nearer and to sit with us even for a few minutes. He came closer and sat by Mother's side, looking at his watch, but said nothing.

I opened my mouth. He was not looking. I opened my mouth again and said loudly, "Ashraf!"

He looked at me.

"It's noisy here. Can you hear me?" I asked nervously.

He shook his head, eyeing me.

I shouted once more, "Happy returns to you!"

He shook his head again. "I can't hear you!"

"This wedding party, is it good? Is it different from wedding parties in Britain?"

He looked at me again. I found myself whispering involuntarily, "I love you."

He looked at me again and said, perplexed, "What did you say?"

I whispered in despair, "Nothing."

He did not hear me. He did not.

"I have to leave." He stood up, looking at his watch.

Mother rose, saying, "We will come with you. Let's go, girls."

When we got back to Ashraf's place, Kareem said, as he sat at the elegant dining room table, "What a boring wedding reception."

I hastened to add, "It was too noisy, wasn't it, Ashraf?"

He took off his jacket and threw it on the chair and sat down recklessly. He didn't answer. He loved the idea of being the darling, desired by all. He is as rare as pistachio nuts: everyone craves them. That's why he visits us. That's why he accepted the invitation and attended the wedding of Abla. It was his pride and arrogance.

Father was sitting opposite Kareem. Ashraf said, "Yes, it was noisy. What were you saying earlier, Wafaa?"

"I was asking if this wedding reception was different from British ones," I said, struggling to conceal my shyness.

"Yes, it's different from British wedding receptions. People here are happy," he said in an enticing voice.

"Do you love Egypt more than Britain?"

He contorted his lips sarcastically and said nothing. Like a king inspecting his subjects, Ashraf surveyed us.

"Let's play cards, all of us," he said, like a little kid.

"Let's!" Kareem said eagerly.

Father said nothing. I could see his admiration for Ashraf and his money, and I could see his fear of him and his principles. Father wanted me to marry Ashraf. Though his dignity prevented him from behaving like Mother, I could still see that wish in his enthusiasm whenever Ashraf's name was mentioned. Sally sat beside Ashraf while Mother remained standing still, maybe out of astonishment or not knowing exactly what else to do. I couldn't imagine Father playing cards. I didn't know if he even knew how.

I sat looking at Ashraf, devouring him with my eyes again. He looked at me, smiling now and then as he held the cards and dealt them with the zeal of a clever boy.

"Come on, Aunt, why are you standing like that?" he asked Mother gaily.

Father answered with his usual sarcasm, "Manaal is no good at playing."

Kareem and Father laughed, but Mother didn't. She was expressionless. I didn't find Father's words embarrassing at all. As for Ashraf, he eyed my mother for a few seconds, then glanced at Father briefly and smiled in a way I could not understand at the time. Ignoring my father's comment, he said, "Let's play, Aunt."

"I'll make tea," said Mother as she headed for the kitchen.

We started playing. Sally and Ashraf had all the luck. I didn't know how to play. I didn't even try to learn. All I cared about was being near him. He was playing like his life depended on it, like he was staking everything he owned and losing would cost him everything.

He threw down the last card and said defiantly, "There you are. Who won?"

Father surrendered, dejected. Kareem and Sally conceded defeat as well. Ashraf said proudly, "Never mind. We'll play one more game."

I felt slightly sorry for Father and pitied him for his losses. But I was rather proud of Ashraf. So I whispered, "Enough. No more playing. It's not permissible in Islam to gamble."

Ashraf burst out laughing and rejoined, "Why isn't it permissible? Anyway, we're not gambling. We're just playing cards. On the other hand, we *could* gamble. For instance . . ." He paused as if thinking about an important matter. Then he stood up, saying, "You may be right. That's enough."

Father nodded and went to bed. He was followed by Kareem. I wished Sally would leave, too, but she didn't.

It seemed that Ashraf's enthusiasm returned, for he said, "Sally, let's play together: you, me, and Wafaa."

I said shyly, "But I don't play well."

He stretched his legs under the table and whispered to me, "You play very well. You have to concentrate on the game and nothing else, though. Let's play. But if I beat you, what do I get?"

I closed my eyes: the situation was beyond my control.

Sally said, "If you beat her, we make her do all the housework for the whole week."

He looked like he was seriously considering the matter. "If I beat you . . . I don't know: let me think of a punishment worthy of you."

I was quick to rejoin, "Gambling is not permissible in Islam."

He grabbed me by the hand and pushed me into the chair and said, sounding utterly bored, "Sit down."

I could not force myself to stand back up.

Then the game started anew. He said to Sally as he sat beside me, "You know, Sally, Egyptian wedding receptions are so noisy. I couldn't hear anything that Wafaa and my aunt said to me earlier."

After a pause he added slowly and cunningly, "I only heard what was whispered to me."

My heart nearly stopped beating. I stood up, confused, and headed for the bedroom. Had he really heard what I'd said? Had he?

He said, smiling, "Wafaa, aren't you going to gamble with us?"

I told him I was tired, and he bid me good night, to which I whispered longingly, "Good night to you."

∾

Sally suddenly asked, "What did Wafaa whisper to you at the reception?"

He replied as he was dealing the cards, "If you win, I'll tell you. If I win, you'll tell me everything about Ahmed."

"What happens if Wafaa finds out?" Sally asked.

"She won't, but even if she does, I don't suppose it'll matter, because I think she's changed."

∼

I forgot to mention Aunt Aliyya. Have I mentioned anything about her before now? She was the person I feared most in my whole life. She was round. She used to go barefoot and squat on the settee with a black veil covering her white hair. She wore the same gray cape constantly, unless she exchanged it for another gray one. To me she always seemed like a mermaid from the bottom of the Nile: knowing everything and able to do everything.

She watched me in distress while I was saying my prayers, and then she said, "This is wrong. Your prayers will not be accepted by God. This way a hundred devils are accompanying you in your prayers."

I said nothing. I dropped to my knees and then prostrated. When I finished saying my prayers I asked fearfully, "Why, Aunt?"

She said energetically, "When you say your prayers, you have to put the right hand over the left one, like so. See? You shouldn't move them. Your arm should hang down like so every time. Beware, Wafaa."

I nodded in response as I always did with Aunt. She was devout and God-fearing. I learned from her, and I dreaded the torture and pain of the hereafter. She would talk for hours and hours, and I would just nod approvingly out of fear and carry out what she asked. I was not well informed on these matters. She knew everything about the hereafter.

I've always been afraid of everything. I was in fear of losing Ashraf. I dreaded that dormant volcano of destructive feelings inside me. I dreaded Mother and Father and my brother. I feared for Sally and thought constantly about Ashraf.

I considered confiding these devilish fantasies to my aunt, but I was afraid. As I was giving her a hand in the kitchen I said, "Do you know about my cousin Ashraf? Has Mother told you about him, Aunt?"

"Your mother tells me nothing."

"He is very good-hearted, but he has sinned. He is acquainted with a loose girl who is, naturally, exploiting him. He is very rich and young. I mean, he has a prominent position."

She shot back dismissively, "May God protect us. Stay away from him, Wafaa. He is impure. He has come from a country that we ask God to protect us from. In that country women commit all kinds of sins. Not like us."

I opened my mouth to say something but I couldn't.

She continued, "In that country they have no shame or fear. There are no girls there. They are all women. Stay away from him, Wafaa."

I hastened to rejoin, "I have nothing to do with him, Aunt. I don't think about him at all. In fact, he wanted to marry me, but Mother has not responded to his request yet."

She made a sucking noise and said, "The first thing he'll do is betray you before your own eyes with one woman or two. Beware, Wafaa."

"God may guide him onto the right path."

"No. God does not guide such creatures onto the right path. The torture and punishment awaiting him in the hereafter are severe." My aunt spoke as if she were in direct contact with God. She acted as if she alone knew everything. I could not argue with her.

⁓

But Ashraf's life was not all pleasure and glory. This was what happened one sunny, beautiful day.

Lubna's brother Ismail ran his right hand over the block of hashish hidden in his pocket, like a hen wishing to be reassured about its eggs. With the left hand he groped for the knife, again like a hen!

He entered the bank, looking for the rich man who had brought shame to his family.

Ismail noticed a young man in jeans and a white shirt. A woman pointed at him, saying, "That's Ashraf."

He looked at Ashraf with a mixture of disgust and fascination. He envied Ashraf for his money. He gazed at his magnificent pair of leather shoes. How he wished to be that elegant! Of course, that was how Ashraf had managed to seduce his sister. He glanced at his own jeans. And the flowery patterned shirt. What a difference! Ashraf, who was far more handsome and elegant than he would ever be, despised him and looked down on his family. He had used all that glitter to exploit his sister. He stared at him as he was conferring with the bank manager, saying "Yes. I understand. You have to watch it. But you have to take some risks. This is what this bank lacks. The stock exchange, for instance, has made some people extremely wealthy. It made some others poor, naturally. But it made more rich people than poor ones."

"Ashraf Daawood, I am here to speak to you."

Ashraf looked at Ismail, astonished, and waved him into his office. "What is it you want from me? Have we met before?" he said with his usual smile.

Ismail reached for the knife. He produced it with the speed of a professional. "I am here to kill you. Do you think you can mock us, and we'll just stay put and be quiet? Do you think you can buy our honor with your money?"

Ashraf looked confused. "Your honor? Yours and whose?"

Ismail waved the knife around. "Don't mess with me. You are having an affair with my sister, Lubna."

"Are you Lubna's brother?"

"I will kill you and kill her, the whore."

Ashraf looked at him, pretending to be shocked, "Do you have suspicions about your sister? What's your name?"

Ashraf examined his face and noted the dark circles around his eyes. He continued with the same false sincerity, "You ought to be ashamed of yourself. Do you have doubts about Lubna? She is the purest girl I have ever laid eyes on. Lubna? The one who works day and night so that you may be supplied with that damned substance that you take and who feeds you and your whole family? You dare to think she is having an affair with me?"

He remembered that he had heard these very words and witnessed this very scene in an old Arabic film. Sometimes old films come in extremely handy, he thought.

Ismail's voice came at him, shrieking and agitated, "Don't insult my intelligence. I *know*. I saw her leaving your apartment at midnight."

Ashraf shrugged his shoulders, displaying his puzzlement. "She handles publicity for the bank. She's not a child. She's equal to a hundred men. Do you want me to swear that my relationship with your sister is nothing more than a working relationship? Lubna is the most honorable woman I have ever seen. You ought to be ashamed of yourself. Aren't you ashamed of yourself? You should be, for having these doubts about her."

"I will kill both of you."

"Do whatever you want, but how will you survive afterward?"

"She won't buy me with her money. I'll live with my head held high."

Ashraf smiled sarcastically and said, "Hold your head high, brother. Nothing that may shame you has happened. Had we had an affair, she would have been among the richest of the rich. But you can see she's still poor. Had she desired money, she would have gotten it. But she is a decent human being. How can I describe her? She is a woman of principles."

Ismail sounded slightly uncertain as he said, "I don't believe you."

Ashraf stood up nonchalantly and said, "Believe me, Ismail. What are you studying now? Your name is Ismail, isn't it? When you finish your studies I hope we can work together. Do you like pistachios, Ismail? Have some, so that we share some food together." He produced a bag of pistachios from his desk drawer and offered it to Ismail, who didn't take it.

Ashraf patted his shoulder and said, "Take it, brother, and join me for lunch. I'll tell you how strong your sister is and how she's involved in the struggle against injustice and corruption. What about you? Do you have political leanings?"

Ismail was revealed as simple, poor, and an addict.

After eating lunch with Ismail in a superb restaurant, Ashraf said, "Now I want to see your apartment."

He drove his car across Imbaba, looking like a child visiting a zoo for the first time. He was determined to go with Ismail because he wanted Lubna. He was playing a game and winning. He felt an extraordinary longing for her.

He looked around him at the open sewage that flooded the street; no one seemed bothered. People walked around looking submissive and dejected. The old shabby rags hanging from the washing lines of the balconies revealed extreme poverty. The buildings looked like they might collapse at any moment.

He saw the old house and the narrow stone stairs and covered his nose with his hand to shield himself from the rotten smell that filled the place.

He entered Lubna's house. The walls were not just dilapidated; they were filthy as well. The gray paint testified to the passage of long and difficult times. The smell of the food Lubna's mother was cooking at the time would haunt him for years to come. He ate nothing that day.

When Lubna entered the room she looked at him in panic. He smiled and said, "I have come to meet your family. Ismail and I have become friends, isn't that right, Ismail?"

～

As she sat beside him in his car she said venomously, "What do you think of our apartment?"

"It's disgusting. How do you live there?" he said through his smile.

"You don't show even a bit of courtesy to me? And what about this relationship with my brother? Do you want to taint him as well? He's a model student. He and the likes of him will change everything."

"Yes, he is an example of a struggling young man. How much is his monthly pocket money?"

"I give him money regularly," she said proudly.

"Are you an idiot, Lubna? Do you really think he is a model student?"

"Yes. He may have his lapses, but at least he's not the rich type who enjoys the wealth of others," she insisted.

"This is envy, then."

"You think I am envious of you or of the rich?"

He stopped the car and said impatiently, "I don't know. Can we change the subject? Listen, let's go somewhere quiet and have a drink. What do you say?"

She nodded. They found a café along the Nile. She followed him in. She tapped her feet as was her custom as she sat.

"Do you despise poverty?" she hissed suddenly.

"I don't like it."

"Do you despise me, then?"

"I love you."

She looked at him with desire and whispered, "You've never said that before. Do you really love me?"

"Yes. I have never loved anyone this way before."

"You haven't asked me to marry you. Why not?" she asked.

He whispered tenderly, "I don't know. I guess I was waiting for the right moment."

"If you really love me, don't you want to live with me forever?"

"I don't know whether I want to live with you forever or not. All I know is that I love you and would like to make all your dreams come true—except the one about establishing a communist state," he said, staring at the water.

"You can't make my dreams come true. No one can," she said, meekly, for the first time. Then she continued, "Ashraf . . ."

"Yes."

"This place is full of rich people. This tea is very expensive. I want social justice. The price of this tea is enough to feed an Egyptian family for two days. Five pounds for a cup of tea? It isn't fair. Injustice can't last forever."

"I just hope I will be able to enjoy something with you. Anything," he sighed.

Lubna left Ashraf's place at about two in the morning. She never made it home. Her mother looked for her everywhere for days. Ashraf was extremely worried because he had not heard from her. Then he found out that his sweetheart was among a group of political detainees. He was confused and furious.

A day or two later, another feeling crept into him: helplessness. He had never before felt so helpless. He had never felt such love and yearning as he did for that Egyptian girl.

4

HE WAS OBVIOUSLY under extreme stress as he was talking to Ismail. "What do you mean, you don't know where she is? What prison? What are they doing to her? You can't abandon your sister like this. Do something. I'm going to do something."

Ismail glanced at him, feeling rather agitated and helpless. He said nothing.

Ashraf left the office early.

This was unreal. She couldn't just disappear like that without a single word.

He went home and put on his best suit. He was boiling with fury. He left his home determined to see a senior army general whose name he had heard from a friend of his aunt's family.

The army man was an assistant to the minister of the interior. Ashraf asked to see him, introducing himself to the secretary as working in the British Embassy in Cairo and saying he was bringing a message from the embassy. Ashraf produced his British passport as evidence. He was allowed to enter the office of the minister's assistant.

Facing the man, Ashraf demanded firmly, "Where is Lubna Thaabit?"

The man looked amazed. "Who's she? And who are you, anyway?"

"She is a journalist, and I am a human being. How can a person be detained for merely thinking, for merely having a different opinion?"

The general stared at him for some time, then said quietly, "You lied. You're not from the embassy. You just happen to have a British passport. You've cheated your way in here. Please leave with no further trouble."

"I just want to understand," Ashraf said firmly.

"You are just a fraudulent Egyptian citizen. I have no time for impostors. Leave before I bring charges against you."

"Why? Why has she been arrested?"

"We object to foreign intervention in our internal affairs."

"You were addressing me as an Egyptian."

"I don't know who this girl is. If someone is arrested it's because they're creating a disturbance at a time when we need people to stand together to achieve peace."

"And what has Lubna got to do with that?"

"I don't know. She may be advocating antipeace policies. Or maybe she was preaching some deviant ideas. Anyway, we are at a very critical point now. The safety and security of our country are the most important things. All detainees will be released soon."

"I don't know where she is."

The man stood up, saying, "I don't have time for this. She is certainly with the other detainees. Visits will be allowed soon. Leave this office now, please."

It was a useless meeting, Ashraf thought. When he left the building he was furious. He felt confused in a way he never had before. It was as if he was experiencing his Egyptianness for the first time.

∿

He sat in front of the TV. His eyes were glued to the car race on the TV screen, but he wasn't really watching.

In his mind he could see terrifying and horrible images of Lubna in the women's prison of Torrah: the toilets, the food, the horrible smells, the boiling heat, and the humiliation. All that humiliation, and here he was, totally helpless—incapable of helping her.

He held the pistachio plate, glanced at it, and then dumped the pistachios on the table. He stared at the pistachios scattered all over, with each piece choosing a spot for itself. He felt a terrifying loneliness that reminded him of the loneliness of his childhood and adolescence. It brought back his loneliness in the British boarding schools and his feeling of estrangement. With the passage of time, his loneliness became something he was used to rather than something he hated. And since it was familiar, loneliness became likable. He felt that was the case with every human situation. It had to pass through the three stages: hate, familiarity, and then love.

~

Take me, for instance: I used to hate archaeology. I then got used to it and later just loved it. But I was so different from Ashraf. Poor him: he had an amazing ability to dislike everything.

~

When the telephone rang he replied in a confident voice, "Yes."

"Ashraf, my darling." His mother's voice had a rattle to it.

"How are you, Mother?"

"How are you doing, my darling Ashraf?"

His mother fell silent as her tears streamed down her cheeks. Ashraf said nothing.

"What's wrong with you, sweetheart? Are you taking after your father or what? Why don't you come back, dear?"

"I'm coming soon, Mother."

"On your own, Ashraf. Understand? You come on your own. I need you, darling. Leave this infidel woman of yours and come home to me. Don't ruin your future. My heart is burning for you. Are you still seeing her?"

He did not reply.

She continued angrily, "You'd better watch out. Don't you fall in love with her. Is she the first one ever? Don't you remember Emily and all the others? You'll soon forget her. Later, if you want to get married, you have Wafaa. She'll cherish you and rear your children."

He heaved a deep sigh and rejoined, "Pray for me, Mother."

"What do you want?"

"Everything."

"Is the girl with you, Ashraf?"

"The girl is in prison," he said firmly.

"Prostitution, of course."

"Politics."

"Of course it is for prostitution. Do you want to marry a convict, my darling?"

He had never told his mother that he wanted to marry her. He had no idea how she had figured it out. He wanted to marry her, and he wanted to marry her now. But he didn't feel like arguing with his mother. The sound of her sobs was torturing him; it reinforced his sense of helplessness. He hated politics, overcrowdedness, and Imbaba, with the exception of Lubna.

⁓

Sitting in our house, he buried his face in his hands as if completely incapable of movement.

I smiled to myself and hoped that Lubna would never be released from prison. That was the punishment that licentious women deserved.

"Ashraf, you cannot remain in this state forever. You have to go back to work. You tried. You tried your best," my mother whispered.

He nodded in agreement and cast a sudden look at me. I couldn't contain my obvious smile. I felt an extraordinary comfort. It was not right to gloat over other people's misery, but licentious girls deserved to be burned alive.

He didn't speak to me, nor to Sally. He was silent and miserable. It made me happy, and I wondered why. Though I loved him, I felt a wild desire to witness his pain and misery, especially since he had failed to mention, even in passing, that day when we were in my room. It was as though he had never touched me or done anything to me. It was as if I were once more living in a daydream.

I returned to my room. I threw myself on the bed and dove into the delicious sea of my dreams. Lubna's predicament made that day's dream even more beautiful. I had been right all along. All my principles won the day, eventually. I sighed deeply as I buried my head in the pillow, dreaming that my sweetheart was whispering to me, "I love you, Wafaa. I love your innocence, your religious beliefs, your beauty, and everything about you. I love your tremor as I kiss you, your shyness when you look at me. I love your virginity and your purity. You are purity itself."

⁓

But you all know that life is treacherous. There's got to be a reason for that. Whenever I overheard my younger sister talking to her boyfriend on the phone I would feel extremely jealous. Then I would feel a burning desire and longing for Ashraf.

One Tuesday I was once more listening to Sally's love whispers. I left my room and headed for the living room, where the telephone was. My heart was pounding as I heard the words, "My wish is to be with you forever. Of course I love you, Midhat, my darling."

I opened my eyes wide as I scrutinized the voice, hearing the name Midhat for the first time. That was not Sally. It was Mother.

It was my mother.

I don't like to talk about this subject. I don't even like to remember it. But there we were.

My face turned red. My cheeks felt like smoldering embers. What I had just heard could not be true. It must have been one of my dreams. Of course, it must have been.

The lofty edifice of my principles had just suddenly collapsed. My mentor and teacher was an adulterer, then. The woman who had instilled in me all those principles was a hypocrite and a cheat.

I would face her with the facts. I would never respect her again. There was no reason in her life for such a disgraceful relationship. And with whom? Midhat, the senior army officer, the family friend. I would expose both of them. I would shame them. But then again, maybe it was an innocent relationship. Of course it was an innocent relationship. False accusations were unfair. What did she say exactly? She said that she loved him. That didn't mean anything, did it?

I dragged myself toward my room. I fell on the bed to restore my breath. I wanted Ashraf. I needed him.

I stopped thinking altogether. I just headed for the telephone. I looked at it, terrified, as if it were a ghost about to pounce on me at any moment. My mother was no longer in the room. I dialed the number, with my lips moving as if reciting under my breath a familiar song. On hearing his voice I whispered desperately, "I need you now."

"Is there a problem? I'm busy at work right now."

"Please, Ashraf, please," I entreated.

"Fine," he said hesitantly.

I gasped, stunned. My face turned white again. Inside me everything seemed to twist and shrink into nothing. I went to the kitchen. When Mother saw me, she said quietly, "Do the washing up, Wafaa. Your father will be back soon."

Avoiding her eyes, I clutched a blunt knife.

I had to cut something.

So I started tearing out the pages of some heavy books.

That didn't quench my thirst.

I stabbed the desk, the wardrobe, but that gave me no satisfaction.

I wanted to stick the knife into something soft, something alive and fresh. I wanted to feel it, to get comfort from it, to hold fast to it. Then I stuck the knife in my arm. No blood spilled; the knife was blunt. I worked diligently and slowly at cutting my arm. Pain comforted me like nothing else. I stopped after a while as I saw blood running slowly and efficiently, like ants leaving their hill.

I buried the knife under my pillow and fell onto the bed, waiting for Ashraf. I didn't cry.

Sally entered the room. She was chattering loudly and energetically. I was pretended to be asleep and said nothing.

At long last the doorbell rang. Sally opened the door cheerfully and called out loudly, "It's Ashraf, Mother."

I got up hurriedly and went to the door. I looked at him imploringly: my savior, my darling. Our eyes met. Faking a smile, he said to Sally, "Is it possible to have some tea? The drive was very long."

Sally raced out. He walked into the living room. He sat in a chair, waiting for me. I had taken off my robe and put on a white blouse that covered my arms. I headed toward him. I looked in his eyes, closed the door behind me, and whispered in a dying voice, "Ashraf . . ."

I saw his eyes shoot suddenly toward my arm, to the spot where blood was soaking my white blouse.

"Why have you done this?" he asked, frowning.

I was breathless then. Ignoring his question I said, "Your aunt. Your aunt, Ashraf, my mother. You have to stop your aunt, Ashraf. Please. Help me."

He looked me up and down as if he had no idea what I was talking about and was trying to figure it out. "To begin with, take it easy," he said forcing a consoling smile.

I sat, saying submissively, "Certainly. By all means."

"So you found out about her relationship with Officer Midhat?"

"You knew about it?" I caught my breath in panic and frustration. My limbs were numb. He had known the whole time and had done nothing. "You did nothing. Why? How did you know? How far have they gone?" I whispered through my suffering.

"In these cases nothing can be done. It is obvious, Wafaa, that your parents' relationship is not ideal. Haven't you noticed it?"

I came nearer and held the back of his chair, saying, "Threaten her. Stop her. Otherwise, I'll tell Father."

"You can't do that," he said severely. "Just cool it. If you face her she'll deny everything. She may even hold faster to him. Close your eyes until it passes. Do you understand what I'm saying? Her desire for him will soon fizzle out, and everything will go back to normal."

"Her desire for him!" I screamed contemptuously. "Oh, my God! She is your aunt. Do you think she has gone all the way with him?"

"Yes, all the way." He smiled bitterly.

"She may be merely in love with him but is resisting his advances. Maybe she has done no more than talk with him."

He looked at me as if I were a naïve child, then said confidently, "Wafaa, when a woman loves, she does not resist, especially if she is married. Do you understand?"

"I don't understand you. You have come from a country of adultery and treachery."

"So it has come to needling and slander. I'd better go. I'm not here to defend myself. Your mother made a mistake. But it's not up to you to judge her. This is none of your business. It's about her relationship with her husband. You know nothing about her relationship with him."

Sally brought the tea and said, smiling, "Here's the tea. Enjoy, Ashraf."

For the first time tears streamed down my cheeks. Sally looked at me, terrified, so Ashraf said, "Go away, Sally. Close the door behind you. Don't eavesdrop. I'll find out what's wrong."

He watched me as I cried. He didn't move a muscle. He just said, "Why are you crying now? Why do you torture yourself? I told you, this is not your responsibility. Pay attention to your studies and forget all about this stuff."

I started to wipe the tears with the back of my hand. Then he opened his arms and said, with some affection, "Come here, Wafaa."

Well. This was certainly no dream. He was asking me to throw myself into his arms. He had done it; I'd heard it with my own ears. This was what I had been dreaming of every day. The dream was realized. He wanted me in his arms. Fate was not so treacherous then.

For a few seconds I was totally confused. All colors, smells, and events became mixed up in my head. I lost confidence in everything. All I wanted were his arms and his embrace.

My eyes were glued to the floor. My tears dried up.

"Wafaa, come over here. You need a friend to hug you," he whispered.

A friend? Had he said a friend? The traitor. What did he mean by an embrace from a friend? An American embrace like the ones we see on TV? The traitor!

It was as if he had awakened me from a beautiful dream. I shook my head as if I were waking up again and then said, firmly, "No. No, I can't."

He dropped his hands over the chair and said quietly, "Well, I think it's better that you ignore this matter completely. I'm sure your mother will end the relationship soon, for your sake and for the sake of your siblings and your father. This is not the end of the world. However, you must learn from her mistakes. Take me, for instance. My father's had many affairs. He still has many affairs. I pity my mother, and sometimes I feel fury toward my father, but it's out of my hands. It's not my responsibility. I'm not responsible for mankind. Anyway, this will teach you to take your time before having a relationship with any man and to form a clear idea about the aim of a relationship and its possible consequences. I say this, though, I'm sure you won't be hasty."

He stood up, glancing at his watch. "I have to go now. They have allowed me at long last to visit Lubna."

"You talk to her. Confront her. Tell her that I know everything," I said sharply.

"I won't threaten her. I told you that's a silly approach and will lead nowhere."

"Threaten her, or I'll do it, and I'll threaten him as well. I'll expose him before the minister of the interior, before all his colleagues. I'll tell his wife and children. Don't think I'm a weak person. I may look it, but when someone tries to destroy my principles . . ."

He went toward the door saying, "Take it easy. I'll think about it and contact you next week."

"Today. You talk to her today."

"Listen to me: let's give her a chance to end the relationship."

"And if not?"

"Give her a month or two."

"I can't."

"That's an opinion. Incidentally I think you need to see a doctor," he said as he opened the door. Embarrassed and feeling ashamed of myself, I fell silent.

"Is this the first time you've done this?" he asked in an emotionless voice, pointing at my arm.

I said nothing.

"You need to see a doctor. This is not a real problem. We all pass through crises, Wafaa. What's important is that you see a doctor."

He left the room, closing the door behind him.

⁓

The minute he was outside the room, Sally grabbed his arm and asked, "What happened between you and Wafaa?"

He saw his aunt preparing lunch mechanically and said to Sally, "Wafaa has a problem at school." He smiled and said, "And how are you, Sally?"

"I met him yesterday. I love him dearly, Ashraf," she said, having forgotten all about Wafaa.

"Good. May you be in love with him always," he said flatly.

"Wafaa no longer spies on me. She doesn't even care about it. She has changed, as you said she would."

Placing the last plate on the table, his aunt said, "Lunch, Ashraf."

"No thanks, Aunt. I have to get right back."

His uncle came out of his room wearing his striped galabiya and walking slowly. He sat at the table and said, "Come over here, Ashraf. We haven't seen you for ages. Kareem needs your advice on a few things."

Before he could respond, his aunt called out, "Wafaa, come here. You've given me no help whatsoever."

Ashraf put his hand on her shoulder and said, "It's okay, Aunt. Leave her be these days. She's having trouble at school."

"By God, son, I'm tired. I live just for the welfare and happiness of the children," she sighed, distressed.

Ashraf half-smiled and rejoined, as he sat in front of Sally, "I know you're a great mother."

"God bless you, Ashraf, you always console me," she smiled and then called out once more, "Wafaa."

Ashraf looked at the long dining table, at his aunt's family, at the husband eating innocently, at the son talking endlessly about every profitable project, and at Sally, who ignored everyone and everything, fully immersed in love. He didn't eat and said little.

⁓

At long last I left the living room. My eyes were full of contempt for Mother. My eyes met Ashraf's as I heard Father calling, "Come here, Wafaa, and eat something, girl."

"I've already eaten," I said in a tired voice.

Ashraf rose, not having touched his food. "I really have to go now," he said.

He then kissed Mother in his usual tender way as if nothing had happened. I couldn't understand how he could do that, how he could control the feelings of contempt inside him.

"Is that all, Ashraf? Won't you have lunch with us? And you have driven such a long way, my darling!"

He left, leaving me behind, standing there holding myself together. What had he said? He'd said, "Come over here," and I had refused. How much I regretted that.

I went back to my room and buried my face once more in my pillow.

I embarked on a new daydream: Ashraf, once more. He came to me, and I told him what I had heard. He seemed really moved. He then confessed his love to me, whispering, "I will take you far away from this house. We'll get married and leave this house forever. I can protect you. I'll take care of your mother's problem. She'll leave that man, I promise you. I'll talk to him, man to man. I'll threaten him, and she will leave him. Come over here, darling, and give me a hug."

He said it: "Come to me." He then held me, and I cried softly in his arms and went into a deep sleep.

⁓

My favorite hobby became hurting myself with a blunt knife, once or twice every day, and then having beautiful daydreams. As for my relationship with my mother, I would rather not talk about it. Whenever she approached me or talked to me I felt a sharp pain in my chest. My heart would pound louder, as if it were on the verge of bursting out of my chest in a revolt against me and my mother. But I'd better not talk about that. It was Ashraf who was important, and this is his story, not my mom's.

In fact, there was no real difference between me and Lubna. Both of us were distinguished by rigidity and by the inability to see each other's point of view. Lubna was living her life, while I was a mere spectator watching the performance from a distance. However, she was also feeling guilty. She was endlessly trying to justify herself before Ashraf and before herself as well. And though she pretended to be a modern girl, she went to Ashraf's place desiring him as he desired her. She didn't go there for any innocent purpose. The fire was burning inside them while she was in prison. He was waiting for her release from prison so he could crush her ribs with his embraces and release into her all his worry and anguish. She was waiting for her release from prison to extinguish her fire of desire for him, her doubts about him, and her fears for him. As for Ashraf, he had made his decision.

He knew what he wanted.

As for me, I started to have doubts about my beliefs. I began comparing Ashraf to my aunt Aliyya, endlessly, as if there were a war between Ashraf and my aunt. I wanted Ashraf but not my aunt. I was like a child whose parents would offer him castor oil or baklava sweets filled with pistachios and honey. The child had to choose, and Ashraf was the baklava with pistachios. My yearnings were about to push me to him to offer him my body for nothing in return. I wanted to knock on the door of his apartment and whisper desperately, "Take me. Let me feel your arms around me even if only once, so that you fill me up and I become part of you. Afterward you may desert me if you wish, or you may just kill me once and for all."

I would then seek the refuge of God from the temptations of the devil and just suppress my yearnings, but I couldn't suppress my imagination. I hated myself for these filthy feelings that no respectable girl should entertain. Were we then talking about respectability? Adultery? Mothers and fear?

He'd said it to me decidedly, "When a woman is in love, she does not resist."

What did he mean by that? If he was aware that I loved him, did he expect me to surrender my body to him? Yes, that was what he expected. Yes, that was why he was angry with me: because I didn't give myself to him. But could I do it?

I sighed deeply as I held the blunt knife. The question reverberated in my head: Can I do it?

I wanted him so much and so badly. I wanted to give myself to him. But what if he didn't want me? What would I do if he did want me? And what would happen after I surrendered to him?

How would I face myself?

How did Mother face herself? What hypocrisy . . .

God help me, but I couldn't do it; I could not suppress my feelings and I couldn't give myself to him.

I stabbed myself repeatedly with the blunt knife while images of Mother, Ashraf, and Aunt Aliyya passed through my mind.

～

A few days later I called Ashraf.

Fury against Mother was oozing from my ears like smoke. I whispered hopefully, "May I see you?"

"I'm busy, Wafaa. Lubna may be released tomorrow," he said impatiently.

"Please, Ashraf," I interrupted him. "I need to talk to you about Mother. I'm afraid for her."

"Don't you have girlfriends? Talk to one of them," he said calmly.

I fell silent briefly before saying, "Yes. Maybe so. Thanks anyway."

I didn't hang up, and neither did he.

After a while he said, "You know, Wafaa, it would be better for you to pay attention to your studies and forget about your mother's affair. Your life is just starting."

"I'd rather be dead than hearing this."

He seemed to smile, and added, "You know, when I was a child I used to dream every day that my mother had just killed my father, then she would stay by his body crying her eyes out. I know how you feel. I know the feeling of estrangement that sweeps over a person when he has lost a parent. It's a form of bereavement and loss, I believe. When I was a child I used to feel despair and fear the way you do, but I never clung to one person in particular."

"What did you cling to?" I asked eagerly.

"I don't know. To myself, I suppose."

It was the first time he had ever opened up to me. My happiness was indescribable. My hope and enthusiasm were boundless.

"And now?" I asked hopefully.

He paused briefly and said: "I cling to myself and myself alone. That's what I learned in Britain. If you don't help yourself, no one else can help you. That's what everyone around me in Britain kept telling me. And you can help yourself."

"I can't. Not when she keeps on seeing and meeting him," I said, almost crying.

"Relationships last only for a limited time," he said firmly.

"Does that include your relationship with Lubna?"

"Even with Lubna," he rejoined, smiling.

"Don't you believe in eternal love? Women are created to be loyal, loving, and giving."

"That may be so. I don't know. But man was not created for those three purposes."

He was serious, maybe for the first time ever and maybe for the last time as well. He was talking to me as if he knew me well. He may have regretted it afterward. How would I know? He may have forgotten his words. Who knows?

There was a pause. He then said softly, "Look after yourself, Wafaa. See you soon."

I sighed deeply as I threw myself on the cushion. If only he had given me the chance to prove to him what love was. If only he would give me a chance.

～

He knocked on the door. He had never felt so much tension before. What had happened to her? Had they tortured her? He would never be able to live without her, ever again. Lubna's mother opened the door and said mournfully, "Welcome, son. Lubna is in her room."

He did not look at the mother or at Ismail, who was seated on the old sofa in the living room, or at the ancient wall. He just walked into her room: he opened the old brown wooden door and went in. She was sitting at the end of the bed, resting her cheek on her palm. The bed was metal, and her face appeared across the metal rods, as if she were still behind bars. He looked at her briefly, came nearer, and whispered bitterly, "Lubna."

She noticed him and quickly said his name.

She had not changed: her eyes were piercing and confident, but their look was unsettled and rather subdued. Her hands were shaking uncontrollably. He walked to her and held her in his arms. He pulled her head to his shoulder and whispered, "I missed you. What have they done to you? Tell me everything."

She opened her mouth to speak, but he added, holding her firmly, "We are going to get married. Today. We will leave this place. I will never see these eyes of yours hurt and dejected again."

She rested her head on his shoulder and said smiling, "I wasn't sure. All this time I have been uncertain whether you love me or not."

He pushed her slightly, saying, "What have they done to you?"

"You asked me before. Nothing," she said calmly.

"I want the truth."

"It was nothing, believe me. Just the humiliation of being in prison. That was all."

"I'll make amends for all that. From today on," he added firmly, "you shall leave politics forever. We'll get married and move away from here. I don't want to hear a single word about politics from you."

She said nothing.

Driven by a sense of moral duty toward Lubna, her brother knocked on the door. He couldn't leave the door closed, despite his admiration of Ashraf. When Ismail was about to open the door, Ashraf rushed over and held it closed, saying, "You can't come in right now."

She smiled and whispered, "You love me?"

"You know the answer. Do you understand what I just said? Your actions and your words change nothing and help no one. Your anguish is misdirected. There is so much anguish inside you, I don't know against whom," he said bitterly.

"Against injustice," she said energetically.

He sat facing her and said tenderly, "No one shall ever be unjust to you as long as you are with me. We will live together. You'll continue writing, but you'll forget all this nonsense and these archaic communist ideas."

"My ideas are not archaic. My ideas will change society. I was not on my own in prison. All those who were there believed in their visions and opinions, too."

He heaved a deep sigh and said, containing his anger, "Let me explain to you calmly: Lubna, I do not like these experiments and adventures, I do not believe that any idea is worth dying for or going to jail for, or even exerting any effort for. The world is moved and operated by capitalism. The stronger ones are those who have more capital. You are just suffering in vain and making me suffer with you, too."

"You're wrong. Capital is not power. There are countries with substantive capital who have no power. It's the West, with its hegemony, that controls everything. I can't abandon politics, Ashraf, after all that I've been through. Do you understand me?" she asked breathlessly.

"No, I don't. I'm fed up with this game. You have a choice," he said sharply. "You abandon politics and marry me and I will lift you and your family from this poverty and wretchedness. You will become a real princess, Lubna, I promise. Otherwise, you lose me forever. I have just a few more weeks in Egypt. Will you come with me?"

She looked at him and their eyes met. She seemed feeble and tiny. He felt a surge of hatred for her beliefs. How could ideas affect people this seriously?

"What is it you want, Lubna?"

"Justice! Have you seen any justice around here?" She said it as if she were a battery-operated doll.

"There is no justice either in Egypt or elsewhere. Justice is a myth invented by man. A myth—no more."

"I will not sacrifice my future for you," she said firmly.

"Your future? What future?" He laughed dryly. "Do you understand what you just said, Lubna? You don't have a future. You live here like a rat in a hole: poor, oppressed, and frustrated. No one knows anything about you. No one will ever know anything about you. People don't care about your ideas and beliefs. Everyone cares only about himself. I am offering you a life preserver, but you prefer to drown."

"All this arrogance!" she shrieked. "I want no life preserver from you, Ashraf."

He opened the door angrily and said, "This is the last time we will ever see one another, Lubna. I don't want to see you ever again."

"Was I begging to meet you? Go. Go to wherever you came from. Go back to the place of injustice—money that is tainted with the blood of the innocent, arms, cheap labor, and banking operations, suspicious deals, theft, usury, and all that other stuff. Go back."

He said nothing and headed for the door. Ismail grabbed him by the arm on the way out of the house, "Take it easy. Let's smoke a joint or two."

Meanwhile, Lubna collapsed on her bed and whispered under her breath, "I love you, Ashraf."

～

Ismail took a long puff from the hookah, which had been laced with hashish. He was calm when he said, "Don't worry about it. I'm sure my sister loves you. She will . . ."

"I know." Ashraf interrupted him tersely.

Ashraf looked in disgust at the colorless flaked chair and the small round table. He breathed the heavy sweat of the clientele of the coffee shop. He felt a compelling urge to throw up. He was feeling a mixture of disgust and fury, which made him uneasy.

Wiping the tip of the hookah nervously, he took a long puff, followed by another and another. He then smiled bitterly and asked, "Ismail, how much money do you need to start having a life?"

"A lot," said Ismail, looking at him in amazement.

Ashraf produced his checkbook and said nervously, "Let's say five thousand. What do you think?"

Ismail looked around and said terrified, "Don't say that around all these people. Otherwise they'll tear you apart as if you were a piñata."

He laughed bitterly and rose, saying, "I feel a mad urge to give you one hundred thousand pounds, but I'll settle for five thousand. Have you ever had such a mad urge? Call it my revenge on her. One hundred thousand pounds means nothing to me."

He held the checkbook and wrote the check for five thousand pounds. Offering it to Ismail, he said, "What are you going to do with it?"

Ismail just giggled in disbelief and said, "This is no time for jokes, Ashraf."

"I am not joking," Ashraf said as he sat down.

Then he held the check out for him and said, "Take it, Ismail, and no more hashish. It will only eat your brain."

"Why?" Ismail asked, stunned further.

"For various reasons," Ashraf whispered.

Ismail looked at him searchingly, "What was it between the two of you? Did you want to marry her?"

Ashraf took a deep puff from the hookah. "Maybe."

"That bitch . . . I'll teach her some manners. She's going to marry you by hook or by crook."

"Are you going to force her to marry me?" Ashraf asked, amused.

"To turn down someone like you? She's a stupid woman," Ismail said with energy and anger.

"How are you going to force her? Tell me," Ashraf said, smiling.

Ismail looked lost briefly. He wasn't sure he could force her to do anything.

Waving the check around, Ashraf asked, "Do you want the money or not?"

"Lubna . . ."

"Forget about Lubna. This money is for you because you're a loyal friend and a protective brother who guards his sister's honor. I respect protective brothers."

"Don't you want her anymore? She is going to marry you. I promise. I'll persuade her."

"No. Don't persuade her."

Ashraf dropped the check on the table and left, saying, "Spend it only on good deeds, my friend."

He felt no regret, but he was rather curious. The following day he learned that Ismail had already cashed the check. That was his final victory over Lubna, Ismail, and poverty itself. Money could do miracles. Lubna had rejected him because she wanted to look after her brother and to rear him out of her own money. She had rejected him on the basis of a principle. She would regret it one day, when she found her brother enjoying Ashraf's money. Money could buy everything. The pride of the poor could also be bought and sold.

He had always believed that.

∿

Ashraf was arrogant and spoiled. Lubna was willful and hysterical. I was quiet and a coward. Ashraf was consumed with anger. He had never expected her to refuse his offer. She was first and last a poor beggar. She lived in squalor. His anger was driving him to travel fast, find another woman, and forget her forever.

Those were days he wished would pass fast.

∿

We didn't see him after he left Lubna. Then he came to our house one Tuesday. I will always hate Tuesdays. He came to say good-bye before returning to Britain.

"I have come to bid you farewell, Aunt. I'm leaving tomorrow," he said as he entered.

I'd known that he would soon go back, but I'd kept on dismissing the idea.

I ceased to breathe for a few moments. I rushed into my room, looking for the knife, which had become my favorite toy. I thrust it into my arm. It didn't bleed, but I felt relieved, though only for a few seconds. I wished he knew how much I loved him. If he knew, he might stay, but then, he might go back to her. Indeed he might.

I heard his voice calling, "Wafaa."

I held onto the door. He was sullen and gloomy. That meant he was leaving alone. Lubna has lost.

I bit my lip and said, panting, "Ashraf."

He looked at me. Mother, Father, and my sister were all looking at me, so I said, sounding muddled, "So, you are going away on your own?"

He nodded. He didn't seem happy. His eyes were full of grief and distress . . . all for someone else. I gathered all my courage and whispered, "There's something I forgot to give you."

He looked at me confused. Then he smiled to his aunt. "Just a minute. Wafaa wants to give me something."

Neither Mother nor Father seemed bothered that I would be alone with him. They knew very well that he had never loved me and never would.

We went to my room. I was tapping my fingers nervously on the desk, and he stood in front of me.

"You have left Lubna because she is a degenerate whore. Is that right?" I asked bitterly.

"No, I have not left her because she is a degenerate whore. I love her, Wafaa, but sometimes circumstances create obstacles for people," he said firmly.

"And my mother? You have done nothing about my mother." I was pushing the books around the table aimlessly.

"I told you to wait. No more than a month has passed since then. Wait."

I held his hand desperately and said, "Don't go away. You can't go away after what you've done."

"I beg your pardon!" He looked stunned.

"You know very well what you've done to me. Do you remember what you said to me in this very room?" I persisted.

He looked at me, examining my face as if I had just descended from outer space. "What did I say?"

I swallowed, breaking into a sweat, and stammered, "You said, 'Do not be afraid, Wafaa. Love is beautiful, Wafaa.' And you said . . ."

He didn't reply. He was silent for a brief moment, then he rejoined, "Yes. Continue."

"And you touched me. Have you forgotten that as well? You touched my face and my arm. Have you forgotten, Ashraf?"

He shrugged indifferently, "I don't know what you're talking about. What I know is that you certainly need help."

"You think I'm crazy?" I screamed in his face.

Mother entered the room suddenly. She looked at me horrified and said, "What happened, Wafaa?"

"Nothing. Leave me alone, please!" I cried.

Ashraf gave her a phony smile and said, "Leave us alone, Aunt."

"You said those words. And you did all that. Yes or no?" I was panting and banging the desk with my fist.

He just looked at me. I had no idea whether he pitied me or not. I couldn't understand the look on his face. He made no reply to my question.

"Yes or no?" I persisted.

"I'm sorry, Wafaa, if I ever did that. I didn't realize . . ."

"Don't say 'if' . . . just confess," I interrupted.

He smiled and said, "You Egyptians love confessions. But any confession extracted this way loses its beauty. Likewise, victory loses its glamour if achieved that way."

"Well," I said, controlling my shivering hand. "You know that I love you—do you or do you not know that?"

"A new confession? I plead not guilty, Wafaa." He was sarcastic but trying to be consoling.

I whispered as tears streamed down my face, "You know."

"I know that you are fond of me," he said solemnly. "But real love will come soon. You'll meet a man who shares your views, beliefs, and background."

"But you touched me. Do you remember? You touched my arm and my face and my hand. Do you remember? Why did you do that? It's not allowed, not possible. It's forbidden. You cannot do that to me if you don't love me," I hissed.

"But you knew I had a relationship with someone else," he said gently.

I interrupted him, "She is a whore. As a man you may need a whore, but you love me, only me."

He heaved a deep sigh, not knowing whether to hate me or pity me. Then he said firmly as he banged the desk, "You need help. You need to see a doctor. Love is not the most important thing in the world. I'm leaving now. I have no time for this. Good-bye, Wafaa."

"Please don't go away," I entreated as my tears flowed.

"I have to go. My work is there. My life is there, and so is my money." He said it as if he were addressing a child.

"I will pay you back for what you did to me!" I screamed angrily.

He opened the door, saying nothing, so I called his name endearingly as I followed him with my eyes.

He probably felt bored by my words, and I might have seemed weak and desperate. So I found myself holding a piece of paper and imploring him, "Are we going to remain in touch?"

"Naturally, my cousin, we shall remain in touch." He patted me affectionately on the shoulder.

"You're touching me again. You did it. Don't lie."

He tried to control his laughter, saying, "You're like a sister to me, Wafaa. Isn't that right?"

I began searching feverishly for a pen among the scattered papers. "I'm not your sister. You know that. I'm not your sister. Where is the pen? Do you have one?"

My mother called out my name, followed by Father doing the same thing, as I was looking for a pen. Ashraf watched me silently as things kept slipping from my hand. I found a pen, which I handed to him with a shaking hand. "Your address. Give me your address."

He took the paper and wrote his address and gave me back the paper. "What are you going to do? Are you going to write to me?"

"Yes. Will you reply? Tell the truth," I said it forcefully, as the tears still ran down my face.

He smiled bitterly. "I've gotten used to this method of orders and interrogations. I don't know whether it's a cultural difference or a trait in your personality, Wafaa. Yes, I will write to you, but on one condition."

"Wafaa . . ." Someone called my name, and I said, "Just a minute," before replying, "What is it?"

"Promise me you'll see a therapist. Everyone comes up against emotions that are too much for them. All of us need help now and then."

"I will. I promise you. But I'm not crazy," I hastened to add.

"I didn't say you were. You're not crazy. But I have to go now." He said it calmly.

"Hug me," I whispered.

"What did you say?" He eyed me startled.

I summoned all my courage and said, "As friends . . . just as you did when you thought I needed a hug. Remember? Yes? Just as a friend. The way they do it in American films."

"No, I won't do it. You don't see me as a friend," he snapped sharply.

"But—" I howled entreatingly.

"Good-bye, Wafaa."

He opened the door and left. He left me behind in my room, longing for his arms, regretting the missed chance, and wishing to be Lubna.

Father came into the room. It was the first time I'd ever seen him concerned. "What's the matter, Wafaa? Is there something going on between you and Ashraf?"

"No. Of course not. I'm just anxious. I used to consider him a brother. I'm okay. It's just that . . ."

"Just that what?" he asked tersely.

"Just that I have to work harder and study for exams. Besides, I'm finding the daily travel to Alexandria exhausting. I'm fine, Father."

He left the room, closing the door behind him. I heaved a deep sigh of relief and buried my head in the pillow to dream as I always did.

～

Do you know the feeling of wanting the impossible and nothing else? That is the treachery of fate. Ashraf was gone, never to return, and I was here. I had to face everything alone, all on my own except for my principles, which I hated. I was here with my adulterous mother, my frustrated sister, a father who was indifferent and ignored everything, and my spoiled brat of a brother. Life was carrying on all around me while I remained living in a dream. I was passive and foolish. I wished I had been like Lubna: daring and revolutionary. But I was just boring, stupid, and crazy as well.

Lubna had lived reality, and I had lived an illusion for a whole year. Lubna had felt him, while I had just dreamed about him. She'd suffered and felt pain, while I had hurt myself with my own hand and enjoyed it.

I should have faced myself and decided what I really wanted; it might even be seeing a doctor, as Ashraf had suggested. But I wasn't crazy. I knew the difference between illusion and reality. I wasn't losing it, although I might have gotten things messed up from time to time. I began to have new doubts about what had actually taken place in my room when Ashraf touched my body. Did he do it, actually? I couldn't tell anymore. Yes, the dream might have merged with reality, somehow, but I was not crazy.

Futility

A man said to the universe:
"Sir I exist!"
"However," replied the universe,
"The fact has not created in me
A sense of obligation."
                    —Stephen Crane

5

NO SOONER HAD HE DEPARTED than I found myself following closely the news of Lubna, as if she were the link between me and him. I wanted to know whether he had contacted her and whether he still wanted her. I did not set eyes on her again, but I read an article she wrote about the abuses of capitalism. Her head seemed full of Thatcher, Reagan, and bananas. She saw communism collapsing because of those three. Was it really vital for East Germany to taste bananas? Were bananas worth all this humiliation? So what if man has to live without bananas? We could live without pistachios and without bananas. But no: the evil Margaret Thatcher and her ally Reagan were leaking bananas as they were smuggling drugs to East Germany and to the Soviet Union.

~

Lubna considered Ashraf to be like Thatcher: a source of corruption, emitting bananas, pistachios, all kinds of luxury goods, and every injustice, and every decadent act, and warmongering as well. Everything, including a kingdom, for a taste of banana. Hadn't Adam been evicted from Paradise for stealing an apple? Man was naturally weak. He wanted luxury. So long as the West offered people bananas bought for nothing from Africa and Latin America, it could control them.

Who said bread and only bread would control people? What about pistachios, bananas, cars, and luxury living?

Luxury living was like a drug you could get addicted to: it would control the cells of your brain, and you could not will it away.

There was enough time for regrets, but Lubna regretted nothing, at first. She was under the influence of a wild wave of fury directed against Ashraf for what he had said to her brother and for giving him money. She wished she could see him and give him a slap that would leave an everlasting scar, like the scar he had left on her.

A few months passed, and the pain began to surface. There was a black hole inside her that had only been filled by Ashraf. And of course there were the intimate moments she had spent with him, which she missed. His touches were getting fainter and fainter in her memory. She had to polish them and try to fill in the gaps with work and anger. For her, Ashraf was different: he was warmth and tenderness. She would remember his tenderness, his fuss over her, his craving for her, and his love. She would remember their screaming matches, which had always ended with hot kisses, the memory of which began to fade. And then his smell—which she had known well—became a distant memory. When he disappeared, regret began. It took various forms: she buried herself in her work, then started to consider marriage seriously. She persuaded herself that she was just missing men and that Ashraf was no more than a male. All men are males. But Ashraf was rich as well, which was a sin. Maybe she was better off looking for a man who had lofty ideals like hers and not one living just to satisfy his personal enjoyment, like Ashraf.

Money was never of any concern to her at all. She'd never liked fancy food, expensive clothes, or even the perfume that he used to buy for her.

Then she began to fall in love with a new thing: power—political power. This love grew inside her every day.

She felt she deserved to have power. She would eradicate corruption and establish justice and fairness. And when power was hers, she would find him once more. She might run into him somewhere. She would be the stronger one. She would torture him and then embrace him and ask him to stroke her hair like he used to. Then she would dismiss him, after giving him that slap on the face that would leave a memorable scar.

⟳

As for me, I consoled myself with the fact that at least I had not offered myself to him. I had only my active imagination.

The difference between me and Lubna is that I was faithful to my wild imagination, while she had her feet firmly on the ground. She could feel the disasters taking place around her, and she could think about her daily bread in the street surrounded by open sewers. How could one live in dreams while the stench of sewage was everywhere?

While she was trying hard to piece together his image in her memory, I used to see him vividly before me, alive and throbbing. Lubna had been in love with Ashraf, and she must have felt immense pride in overcoming her love for him. How stupid of her!

As for me . . .

I held the blunt knife in disgust; what a coward! I could not manage even to die. All my life I had been a mere spectator. I went to the kitchen and took out the knife that Mother used to cut meat. Then I headed to my room. If I stuck the knife in my artery, everything would be over in a few seconds. Then what? I was afraid of the punishment handed out in the grave for sinners and in this life, too. I wanted nothing except him.

Why shouldn't I die? I was useless anyway; both a coward and crazy. But there were small things that tied me to life, things like the train station and the conductor who smiled at me one day and said, "May God grant you success, daughter." I used to see him every day. Whenever I saw him I felt comfortable and at ease. And there was Uncle Saleem with his mature pastrami and olives and strong smell of garlic.

I naturally thought about killing Ashraf. But my cowardice prevented me from killing him before his departure—or it might have been my heart. I wasn't sure. And where could I find him so that I might kill him?

I would have threatened to kill him, but why would he fear me when he knew I was a coward incapable of doing anything? My passivity kept daring me to commit suicide or else to see a doctor, on my own. I hesitated for a long time. Then I wrote him a letter or two. He didn't reply. I was swaying between life and death.

~

The psychiatrist sighed as she said, "And then what?"

Tears welled up in my eyes. "I loved him more than anyone or anything else. I thought about no one else. I dreamed about no one except him."

The telephone rang. The psychiatrist interrupted me to answer the call. "Tomorrow. We want it to be a good party, God willing, darling." She put the phone down and continued, "And then?"

I felt a violent urge to slap her face because she cared nothing for me, for my destiny, and for Ashraf. But my cowardice won the day, as usual. So I replied clearly, "He was in love with a communist journalist. She went to prison, then was released, and they separated. And my mother—Mother had an affair with a police officer. She has not ended her affair. I don't want to see her."

The doctor said sarcastically, "The man you're in love with came from the West. He was decadent and in love with a loose girl to boot. Forget him!"

"I can't."

"Forget him. You may be imagining this affair, the one between your mother and the police officer."

"I imagine nothing. I heard her—believe me," I persisted.

"You need to take a tranquilizer and forget this man."

She then looked keenly at me for a few moments. "It seems to me that he is more than a man."

"What does that mean?"

"Do you have any political affiliations?"

"No. I don't understand politics."

"I see him as the West with all its omnipotence and arrogance, and I see this Lubna as communism—their relationship was a love-hate relationship, a maneuver between the democratic West and communism."

I looked at her, stunned. "What about me?"

"You are the East with its yearning for the West, which cares nothing for it and for its future. You tell me—Ashraf is your cousin? Are you sure he exists? Is he a figment of your imagination?"

"You think he's fictitious, don't you? He's real. He exists. Ask Mother."

"But you are political. You love politics. Do you have specific orientations? What did you feel about the assassination of Sadat? Atrocious, wasn't it? Where were you then? What did you feel—guilt, fear, or grief? The West says we kill our presidents. What do you think?"

"I think *you* have certain political tendencies, although I don't know what, exactly. Ashraf is a human being whom I have loved. He's real. I don't think he's the West or the East," I interrupted her sharply.

She looked at me, as if I were speaking in a language that she could not comprehend, and said nothing.

A heavy silence ensued, and then I said, "What about my wild imagination? What am I to do about it?"

"You have suppressed desires. Maybe you should get married. All men are alike; this Ashraf is not unique. Marry another man," she ordered.

"I can't. I imagine no one else. I see no one else. My imagination takes control of me completely," I said assertively.

"Murder," she said sharply.

"Murder whom?" I asked, looking at her, terrified.

"Your imagination, naturally. Resist it. Do away with it."

"If I kill my imagination, what is there to live for? I live on my imagination. Do you want to deprive me even of that?"

"Imagination is behind all catastrophes, especially ours, we Arabs, we, the developing world."

"Imagination is what is keeping me alive. I could never murder it, ever."

～

Kill it? I hugged myself in panic. The doctor wanted to finish me off. Kill what? What was there to live for if I did? What?

Mine was a lurid imagination; I should be ashamed of myself on its account. It had been maintaining me. It was more valuable to me than anything and anyone except Ashraf. Filthy, petty, or deviant as it might be, it was still part of me. I could not tear it out of myself.

What do we have other than imagination? And they want to deprive us even of that?

So I am the East, which is dazzled by Ashraf's West, Ashraf's pistachios, and Ashraf's culture. And if I am the East, why did she want to deprive me of my imagination?

What is left for us other than an active imagination? Money? Knowledge? Tradition? Ancient civilizations, the opera house? Nile steamers, hotels, expensive restaurants that offer steak with pepper sauce?

What was left for us without imagination?

Aunt Aliyya?

The punishment of the grave?

The various forms of torture?

Martial law?

Mercedes cars?

What would be left for us if I killed my imagination?

I would have a lot left: plenty of fear and oppression. I would heed all orders and follow all rules. I would walk like all the others, with closed eyes, a closed heart, and my slaughtered imagination.

My imagination is what maintains me, what keeps me alive.

It would save me one day.

Cure me with my disease.

I knew that Ashraf was holding me as his captive forever. I didn't know how, but I hoped I would know someday.

My imagination was bound to save me.

Cure me with my disease.

How could I entice Ashraf the way pistachios entice eager fingers?

～

I returned home too much of a coward to die and more eager to meet my death. That day something strange happened.

Father, Mr. Musad al-Mutwalli, came home that Friday. He looked different. The sarcastic, indifferent look that was his mark had vanished and was replaced with the look of a billy goat getting ready for a vicious fight with its enemy, with a stiff neck and pointed horns ready to deliver the deadly thrust.

He shouted at my mother as he entered, "Where is Sally? Where is your daughter, woman?"

I came out of my room. Kareem came out of his. We looked at Father, totally stunned. Mother looked at Father, terrified, and said, "In school, of course. Why are you screaming in my face?"

A battle was about to start or to end, it seemed. No one knew. The lucky one that day was Sally, who happened to knock on the door at that moment. I opened the door for her.

Father shouted at her, "You bitch! Where have you been? I am going to straighten you out and teach you some manners, since your mother knows nothing about what happens around here."

Sally clung to me. She was shaken and speechless. It was evident to me that Father had found out about her relationship with our neighbor. But that relationship was honorable—it was no more than love. I wished I could whisper to Father, "You understand nothing. This shouldn't worry you. You should worry about a different matter."

My train of thought was interrupted by seeing Father taking off his old shoes. Sally closed her eyes, anticipating the fall of the shoe on her face. The shoe fell with a loud noise that was followed by louder screams. But they didn't fall on Sally's face but on my mother's. The others were terrified, but I felt a queer satisfaction. I felt guilty about that, but satisfied all the same.

Kareem held Father's hand and pleaded, "Take it easy, Father. There's no problem. Mother did nothing wrong."

"Please, Father, in the name of the Prophet," Sally whispered.

I didn't ask him to stop hitting Mother. I just retreated a few steps, looked at Mother's face while she was on the floor, and felt a mild suffocation and a frightful satisfaction.

Father didn't stop. He went after her with his shoe, hitting her on her face and her shoulders. She couldn't resist him. She screamed and screamed.

Mother's blondish hair was scattered all over her face. Blood was dripping from her cheek. Almost breathless, he stopped hitting her and opened the apartment's door.

"You want to go? Go then. Go to hell, whore."

He left the room. Sally and Kareem were crying. They supported Mother as she got up. I was watching everything, wordlessly. Satisfaction didn't leave my heart for a minute.

I went back to my room feeling a mixture of puzzlement and guilt. Why did Father do that? Had he found out? Had he always known? Why did he wait to face her, then?

I had never seen Father do anything like that before. Why was he so furious? He hadn't confronted her at all. As for her, she said nothing. She didn't leave. It was as if there had been an understanding between them, with him saying: "I know everything, Manaal. I will not confront you. My pride doesn't allow it." Or, "I don't know everything, Manaal, but I have my suspicions about you, Manaal, and I detest you, wife."

As for her, I don't know for certain if she felt guilt, and she didn't leave. I don't know if she knew the consequences of leaving—she would be left with nothing. Of course, Midhat would not want to marry her. She couldn't even dream of it.

The thing was that I felt that strange satisfaction and felt no pity whatsoever for Mother. Rather, I felt deep love and respect for Father.

Mother knew it. She might have known the reason. In our house, the house of Musad al-Mutwalli, a lot was felt but not articulated. There were silent dialogues shaking the walls of that house every day.

Mother severed her affair with Midhat, or so it seemed to me. The relationship died altogether shortly afterward anyway.

My days passed in slow, depressing monotony. I used to spend most of my time lying on the gold-colored couch in the living room, inspecting the gilt scales on the chair, to the point that I could see golden scales before me whenever I closed my eyes. Life was slipping through my fingers and limbs. No one felt my presence. No one cared about me.

I used to watch Mother in silence, wondering what made her do what she did to us and to Father. I may have always known its reason but ignored it every time.

Father used to treat Mother as if she were an insect. The sarcastic, mocking look never left his eyes. I had never heard him say "Thank you" or "Yes" to her. I had never heard him say anything pleasant to her. He would just listen to her in silence, staring at her with contempt and disdain. When she asked him a question, he would turn his face away, making no reply. She would speak energetically or angrily, but he would not reply.

I had no idea whether her affair with Midhat was a desire on her part to feel important, and to escape the look of contempt and disdain—or if she just wanted to be worthy of Father's look.

It may be both.

I made no excuses for her. I never forgave her. But with the passage of time, I came to understand her reasons.

～

My imagination was playing with me, pampering and tickling me.

I would see myself surrendering my body to him once more. I would feel his kisses, as if they were real, covering me and tearing me to pieces. He was tender sometimes, but cruel at others. In my daydreams I used to see him kissing Lubna with yearning and craving. Then I would see Mother kissing Midhat, and I would shake myself, disgusted, and hate my imagination. However, his image would ultimately take over, and I would feel jealousy and hatred toward Lubna.

"You know, Wafaa, the older I get the more I entertain this strange feeling that all people are just people. They love, hate, err, betray, feel jealousy, and work. I went this year to Turkey, India, and Spain and found nothing more than people. There are various religions, forms, and petty disagreements, but the people are like various types of rabbits, nothing more. Do you know what I mean?"

That was what Ashraf had said one day. The words stayed in my mind as I looked at my aunt holding her rosary and talking, with everyone just saying "Yes."

My aunt used to love walnuts. She used to love cracking them with her teeth as she talked. She once crouched on the gold-colored couch. She held a walnut, put it between her teeth, and pressed hard. I looked at her in panic and pitied the skin of the nut, which she spat out contemptuously. She shouted at the maid, "You, girl, get the broom!" She said to me, "This maid will kill me. I reared her like my own daughter. I bought her a new dress and a pair of shoes and everything. But she can hardly wash two plates. She used to sleep anywhere anytime, like a child."

Without thinking, I said to my aunt, "She's very young, Aunt!"

"Ten years! Ten years old. At her age people used to start a family or build a home."

I never saw Aunt cook. She would just crouch on the couch and change the tablecloth of the dining room from time to time. There was a white cloth with fringe, which she put out when a potential groom for any of her daughters paid a visit, or when a rich relative came. As for the red-striped one, it would be on when we were the visitors. There was a transparent plastic cover, which she used when she expected no one.

"What's the news, Wafaa, of that flamboyant cousin of yours?" She smiled maliciously.

"He returned to Britain," I replied submissively. Her words were like needles pricking my heart.

She rejoined: "God has saved you from him. You must marry a man who protects and cherishes you. I have a suitor for you, an engineer working in Saudi Arabia. Also, Wafaa, you have to attend the religious lessons held at the mosque. I give lessons there now. May God reward me, according to my intention. Do you have anyone giving lessons in Damanhour? What do you think about the suitor?"

My blood curdled at the idea of marrying someone other than Ashraf. It seemed my body desired no one else.

I made her no reply, so she continued, "God blesses him. He is religious and reasonable."

"And why would he want to marry me, in particular?" I asked bitterly.

"He wants to protect a religious girl such as you. A girl from a good family. He knows and trusts me," she asserted, looking at me stunned.

"So he wants to marry me as an act of charity?" I said in despair.

"May God honor and reward him, according to his intention," she said plainly.

I made no reply. I was extremely angry. Had marriage become, in our time, a charitable deed, a religious act, or a sacrifice, or what? And what was wrong with that? Aunt was kind and good-hearted.

I could tolerate her no more. So I got ready to perform my noon prayers.

I resumed observing my prayers. My mind was, however, elsewhere. I felt a strange lack of confidence before God and before my aunt. I was afraid of her comments, of the devils who were surrounding me as I prayed. I was afraid I might make a mistake, afraid of the severe punishment meted out in the grave and in this life. The grave with its torture, darkness, demons, and solitude used to frighten me most. As I prostrated, a tear dropped from my eye. I missed him and was fully aware of the futility of my feelings and of my defeat. I wanted him badly, but I never had my fill of him.

I heard Aunt's voice coming to me again "This is wrong, Wafaa. You are performing prayers incorrectly. There are rules for praying."

I felt a strange urge to laugh. While everyone kept talking about the rules and principles of prayers, about the rituals and the ceremonies, I could see clearly the thin skin under which lay the rotten filth, which was as ancient as history and archaeological ruins. I could see the gilt veneer of the sofa. My aunt was a snob, thinking she was above her own children and their spouses. As for Mother, I wanted to say nothing about her. For a moment I was seized by a fit of wild fury and despair, and I found myself saying with contempt, "Shut up, Aunt!"

She looked at me in a real panic and asked God to protect her from evil.

"Who do you think you are to judge my prayers?" I snapped while still on the prayer mat.

"I am older and more knowledgeable than you are. You have to learn from your elders. Your prayers are unacceptable, Wafaa."

I laughed a dry laugh and said, with tears in my eyes, "How do you know they're unacceptable? Isn't God the only one who knows that?"

"I know."

"Why? Is there someone in heaven telling you?"

"I ask forgiveness of God. You have become an infidel, girl."

Her words silenced me, so I said nothing.

～

Please, Ashraf, just answer me. Say anything. If you do not reply to this letter, I will kill myself. I will do it.

He didn't reply, and I didn't kill myself. I was about to do it, though. I was contemplating the method to use. I'd found it, but many things stood in my way, as I said earlier. I had the knife in my hand. I was in love with that knife. The same love that I felt toward Ashraf. It was the love of the wretched and the desperate.

I would just stick it in my veins, and it would all be over. If I did that I would not go in the morning to Uncle Saleem, the grocer. I would not smell his pastrami.

Also, Aunt Aliyya would be happy to see me dead, naturally. She would think I had committed some sort of sin. I would not give her the satisfaction.

Aunt Adlaat said a lot of nonsense. I didn't have the heart to reply to her. I'd have to reply to her before my death, naturally. There was a lot to settle before death.

However, Ashraf had not gotten married. I knew it. Lubna hadn't won. As for me, I was here sitting and waiting in cowardice. I was dying slowly, for I was torturing myself with a blunt knife.

But if he was somewhere, and unmarried as well, then there was still hope.

I heard the echo of words that found their way to my heart: "Do you believe what you are saying? All you talk about is afterlife torture, demons, and graphic details about torture for sinners. Do you have anything bigger to think about? You're interested in the small details, but who are you? What relationship do you have with God?"

I had not understood those words of his then.

I only understood them when I tasted the pain of impossible hope, longing for one man in particular, with weakness, fear, and despair.

Those were his words, but I didn't know whether or not he meant them.

But God exists. He was close. Always close. As I entertained doubts about my faith, and about whether the devil was controlling me and madness was taking over my mind, I would feel that God was close to me. It was as if he didn't know Aunt Aliyya, or bother about her. It was as if he loved only me.

A new feeling was being born inside me. It might be hope. God's mercy was limitless. My perception of religion had been based on punishment, not on reward. But now I felt a new confidence that despite all my doubts and fears, I was close to God, and he was merciful. I'll have to forgive Mother one day, although maybe not in the near future. I had to believe that I was right all along. Yes. I used to have no self-confidence. I still believed that Lubna was a degenerate. If that was what I believed, then why did I have to state it?

Each one of us has his own reservations, prejudices, and rigid beliefs. But why did we manifest contempt of others?

Like a ray of light, the idea struck me: Lubna was controlled by extremist ideas—equality and communism and so on.

Aunt Aliyya was controlled by an extreme belief in punishment—torture, revenge delivered to infidels, and the like.

I was controlled by an extreme fear of punishment in the grave.

Ashraf was controlled by an extreme belief in the vital importance of money.

Every extreme belief destroys its holder. And every extreme idea is empty and fragile.

Everything around me was changing. I no more feared the punishment and torture of the grave. Rather, I could sense the mercy of God.

∾

I was sitting once again on the sofa in the sitting room. I heard Mother's voice trembling for the first time.

"Why are you killing yourself?"

I looked at her, stunned. She had not said a word to me since Father pounced on her. She used to just look at me with contempt from time to time.

"I'm fine," I whispered as I rested my head against the sofa to stop shaking.

"It's over. Forget him," she said as she sat.

I felt ashamed of myself but said nothing.

So she snapped in anger, "Answer me, girl! Am I not your mother?"

"My mother," I whispered, feeling the pain.

"Answer me! Your sister wants to get married to the boy she loves. It turns out he's a good boy. Do you want her to get married before you do?"

I turned my head away, trembling, and said through my teeth, "Let her get married!"

Our eyes met.

"What is it you want? Have you gone crazy?" she said, examining my face intently.

I was choked up with tears. I said nothing.

"What is it you want?" she screamed.

My tears flowed, and still I said nothing.

"Are you really a daughter of mine? Why is this my luck, and fate, with children, Lord? Please, God, forgive me and pardon me from this grief!" she cried.

She looked at me as I cried silently. My tears seemed to make her angry, pain her, or provoke her. I couldn't tell. So she just continued, "Shut up! You've been acting this way for too long. He doesn't want you. It's time you understood. Just forget him."

I sobbed out loud and whispered through my tears, "God exists!"

She frowned and seemed confused. Then she patted my shoulder slowly and whispered, "That's enough, Wafaa. Enough."

And she left the room.

She had not patted my shoulder that way for ages. I wondered if it was love or mere duty.

I ran to the kitchen, looking for the blunt knife. I couldn't find it. Maybe I didn't want to find it. I went back to my room and whispered, "God exists!"

〜

My sister got married. I saw happiness born out of love shining through her eyes.

My days passed, dull and boring, but my imagination would come to the rescue to entertain me and maintain me.

Sally was different from me; she was daring, strong, and forward. She had a strange method of attracting men. She was infatuated with her husband. But that didn't stop her from being the one always in control. Her coquetry with him was odd. She would act as if she was telling him off or teasing him harshly.

When she gave birth to a boy, she sighed in faked pain and whispered, "I wanted a girl so badly! I am giving you your wish, Ahmed, but I am sad because I wanted a girl."

She acted like she was presenting the baby boy on a silver platter, asking him to pay the price. I knew my sister well enough to understand that she was proud of herself for giving birth to a boy. I saw the fear and love in the eyes of her husband. I have never seen such love or fear in the eyes of any man before.

I used to look at her in utter surprise when she sat at home with Ahmed and the baby boy in her arms. Her eyes were full of pride. Her husband would be looking at her in awe, dazzled. I would see him put his hand tenderly on her shoulder, only for her to remove it in what seemed like a bratty way, saying, "Please, Ahmed, leave me alone. I can hardly bear myself. This boy of yours will cause my death. What made me get married so young? Marriage is such a messy business."

Ahmed would then change the subject.

My sister knew how to deal with men, how to maneuver, challenge, and flirt with them. They were hunters who became victims of their prey.

One Monday she sent him to buy kebab sandwiches. He never came back. He just died. He died all of a sudden while we were busy with the details of living.

〜

I completed my studies. Ashraf was in my mind every moment. He hadn't married yet and hadn't returned.

I didn't dare think about hearing his voice or try to analyze its tone, in case it reflected indifference, pity, or ridicule. Hope inside me was nourished by my imagination.

I was awarded a teaching diploma and got a job teaching at a girls' school in Alexandria. Despite the fact that I was provincial, my pupils loved my stories. My imagination was my salvation. I used to teach history as I saw it, not as it was. I used to tell stories about knights and romance. I felt that my heart was as young as, if not younger than, theirs. Teaching bored me, but I welcomed with pride my salary and my earnings from private tutoring.

One day I just sat and wrote him a totally different letter. This one was full of confidence. I didn't repeat what I had heard from my aunt, my community, or anyone else. The words were mine. I didn't entreat him or beg, like I used to do all those other times.

I wrote to him, once more.

Dear Ashraf,

Do you know that I was wrong about Lubna? I think I just didn't understand her. I think she was in love with you, and that she suffered for being away from you. I believe I was cruel in my judgment. I also believe I will live whether you send me a letter or not.

I will live, as I now earn my own keep. Yes, I am now a teacher of history in Alexandria. Did you know? I commute every day. You may ask, what does history have in common with archaeology and antiques? My answer is, our history has not changed for thousands of years. Our history is antiquity. Do you understand?

I'm helping Father with the household expenses. As imports became difficult, his financial position became lamentable. I also give Mother money for her expenses.

I feel proud of myself. Guess who buys winter clothes for her and for Kareem? Me! Do you believe it? I love Mother now. I love her anew. She loves me likewise.

Do you remember the space separating Mother from Father when they were sitting on the couch? That space is now bridged. My mother bridged the gap by consuming stuffed dishes cooked with butter. Father helped her toward that goal. So no distance now separates their two huge bodies.

As for Sally, you know the full sad story. She married her sweetheart. He died a year ago, leaving her with a son. She is now remarried, a common-law marriage to a well-off man who is already married. She lives in a small house and talks about nothing except the other wife and her bad luck, and how she used to be so beautiful. Poor Sally: she matured before her time. Death is horrible. I fear and hate it.

Will you write back?

If you don't, I won't die.

I will just be very sad indeed. Talk to me.

He did not write back.

You have not written back. It doesn't matter. Have you received my letters? Are you married? Are you happy?

I will marry no one else, Ashraf.

And why has God saved me when I was on the verge of madness? I do not know.

Ashraf used to say, "If you don't help yourself, no one else will," and I would repeat to myself, "If God does not help me, then I will be lost, like a fly in a house sprayed with an insecticide. I am nothing but a timid fly hovering with short wings, above the station of her brain and her heart. I am only an insignificant fly. When I die, no one will bother."

I did not love myself.

I did not admire myself.

I did not like politics like Lubna.

I liked and loved nothing, except him.

Most of the flies that entered the room that had been sprayed with insecticide would die. One or two of them would get away, alive. I was the one who did just that.

My consolation was that he had not married, and that Lubna had won nothing.

6

IN LONDON, it was a sunny, bright, and beautiful day. The moment of confrontation between Ashraf's mother and his father, Dr. Mahmoud Daawood, had come.

When tension already reigned in the traditional English-type household, when any sound, however faint, was enough to excite the raw nerves of those present, Laila, Ashraf's mother, exploded at the dinner table at her husband: "Stop eating. Look at me! Look at me for once!"

"I don't want to see you, Laila," her husband hissed between his teeth.

Ashraf finished his meal as if he had heard nothing. He was used to his mother's eruptions and his father's hatred of her. The whole situation was no longer his concern.

"Who is she this time? A nurse as young as your children?"

"This time I'm going to marry her, Laila. I don't have a lot of time left," he stated coldly.

Ashraf dropped the spoon and looked at his father intently. He saw the hysterical look in his mother's eyes as she screamed, "I will destroy you and destroy this marriage, Mahmoud!"

"It's already destroyed."

"When I first saw you with this decadent English girl, I decided to say nothing. That was for the sake of my darling Ashraf!" she shouted as her tears mixed with her makeup and her gray hair flew all over.

"Exactly," he said defiantly. "It's been over since that day."

"May God take you to his side and relieve me of you."

"Enough of this backwardness," he interrupted her contemptuously.

She grabbed his shirt. Ashraf, who was standing up, saying nothing, had never seen her reacting so strongly. "Me, backwards? You pathetic womanizer!"

Ashraf never liked such scenes. This one was particularly disgusting. So he stood between the two and said firmly, "That's enough! Let's go, Father."

He dragged his father out of the house. They'd walked together a few steps when his father said calmly, "I can't take it anymore. I can't tolerate your mother anymore. Don't believe every word she says. She's imagining these things. Your father is a respectable man."

Ashraf nodded in agreement. As he looked at the dark street, at the asphalt that was everywhere, and at the puddles scattered along the way like foundlings, memories crossed his mind of Lubna, his flat in Zamalek, his aunt, and maybe even Wafaa, as well.

He closed his eyes as he listened to his father. "I wasn't joking. I will leave your mother. You're a man, and you know what I mean. This is the first time I've talked to you man to man. I have tolerated a lot, son, for your sake. All her madness and jealousy. She is a liar. Don't believe a word she says. You are my only hope, Ashraf. You know, I was thinking about buying a new car for you. Do you need a new car, Ashraf, darling? Why aren't you saying anything?"

Ashraf was busy dipping his shoe in the small puddles left by the rain on the street. It was something he used to do as a child, watching for the change in the color of the shoe after it got wet.

"What car do you fancy Ashraf? Tell me: Do you have a girlfriend now?"

He shook his head, absorbed with his wet shoe.

"Are you still thinking about the Egyptian journalist?"

He shook his head once more.

"You are the most valuable thing I have, darling. You don't want to see your father humiliated in this way. Do you see how your mother treats me? I have tolerated it for years, just for your sake."

He said nothing. But suddenly he heard a voice, that of a young man, maybe sixteen: "A light, please."

"Piss off!" Mahmoud said with contempt.

Only a few seconds later, the skinny young man reappeared, accompanied by five others. They surrounded Ashraf and his father. The young man had a big stick. He landed one single blow on Ashraf's father's head. Ashraf struggled with one of the gang, and he managed to throw him to the ground. Their eyes met. Ashraf expected to find hatred there, but he found nothing, so he punched him in the mouth. It was then that he heard his father's scream. He looked around him. The gang had vanished. His father lay on the brightly lit street breathing his last.

Everything had happened so fast.

"Father! Father!" Ashraf shook him, then held his warm hand.

It was a strange situation. A fast death. Faster than the Concorde. It was sudden, funny, silly, and absurd.

He felt everything around him was unreal and make-believe. The truth fell on his mother like lightning. She howled, collapsed, wore black, and said to her son, "Your father was an angel. Mahmoud, my darling, I will not live without you. I will wear black forever. He used to love me a lot. Before his departure he told me, 'There is no taste in my life without you.'"

Stunned, Ashraf looked at his mother. He was totally puzzled by his mother and her surprises, just as puzzled as he was by his father's sudden death.

He sat on his bed in his apartment thinking about his mother and her sudden love for his father, and her wish to live for his memory. At first he thought his mother's reaction was borrowed from her favorite love songs and old movies. A year after his father's death, however, Ashraf began to see things more clearly. His mother was still wearing black. She was still crying and telling stories about how his father was infatuated with her. She would go on for hours, and to anyone she came across.

Is there a stronger revenge?

Rewriting history is the best form of revenge.

Dr. Mahmoud was not there to defend himself or to express his desire to divorce Ashraf's mother and marry another woman. As luck granted the mother an invaluable present, and answered her last wish, she would live rewriting history while he was spinning in his grave, screaming, "I hate you, Laila!"

She would say through her tears, "He was in love with me. He died in my arms." She would smile, cry, thank fate, and lie.

How beautiful lying is! It is sweet, convenient, and crunchy, exactly like pistachios.

～

I wrote to him again, consoling him, and I visited my sister in her new home. I saw the shadows of misery in her eyes. I saw that empty look, familiar in the eyes of the wretched. She was taking her anger out on the other wife, as if she were the one who had snatched Sally's first husband away. She shouted at her son as if he were the one standing in the way of her eternal happiness. I was just listening silently with pity and anger. Until one day . . .

A letter from Britain arrived!

Dear Wafaa,
    Thanks for all your letters.

God had answered my supplication.

The reply had come. It submerged me in a happiness that I had forgotten. So I ate the rice and potatoes that Mother cooked with a relish and lust new to me. I felt life was beginning again. I ate. I enjoyed food. I felt the cold and the heat, and sampled the strong and delicious taste of tomatoes. I took a very deep breath: his reply had arrived. But why?

Why did Ashraf reply? Why now?

Perhaps it was pity for me.

But he had shown me no pity when he saw me going to pieces before him.

I felt my heart tighten, all of a sudden. I made a quick exit. Did he love me? Maybe not. Of course not. But he'd replied to my letter. Why? Curiosity? It might be a sudden sense of duty. He might have been bored stiff with my persistence. It was possible that he'd felt my sincerity and my love, at long last. He might not write again.

It was a very short letter, written in a quick hand. He was probably going home with his girlfriend. He probably took her in his arms, and then remembered the American hug that he'd wanted to give to me and that I had rejected, only to beg him later to give it to me, which he'd refused.

He might never write to me again.

When he woke the next day in the arms of his English girlfriend, he would have forgotten that he had written to me.

He might never write to me again.

So I wrote to him with a pleasure I had long forgotten.

How come you thank me? I love you.

Then I crossed out *I love you* and replaced it with *I love writing to you.*

A few months later I received another letter from Britain.

Dear Wafaa,

In one of your letters you described death as atrocious. Do you remember? I also fear and hate it. Sally's situation saddened me. But I am happy for Aunt, and for the change and vigor that I felt in your letters. I am happy for the words you wrote about Lubna. How old are you now? Twenty-four? Twenty-three? You have matured a lot in the last few years.

I pressed the letter to my heart. I could not contain my happiness.

I had not planned to phone him. I knew I would collapse. I would not be able to say one single word to him. But after his replies to my letters, I felt a strong urge to hear his voice. The first problem was how to get his phone number. The second problem was what he might do on hearing my voice. I could console him for the death of his father.

Faking indifference, I asked Mother whether she had my aunt's phone number. She looked surprised and said indifferently, "In the address book, over there. Why do you want to speak to her?"

I made no answer. My heart was pounding as I waited for dawn to come so I could go to the international call center. When I slept that night, he was with me; he was within me.

"Wafaa?" my aunt Laila said, rather astonished.

"I need Ashraf's number. I have to ask him about some English vocabulary," I hastened to claim.

Did she believe me? Maybe yes, maybe no. But she gave me the number.

⨪

I looked at Sidi Jabir's old international call center. I had never been to one before. I felt I was already nearer to Ashraf, and that I was abroad across borders and airports.

I looked at the center's attendant. My attention was drawn to his sharp features, his hawk nose, and his skinny body. He was Egyptian, an Egyptian in every way. He asked indifferently: "What number?"

I gave him the number. He didn't look at me but said with the same indifference, "Cabin number four."

I stood waiting. I was panting and soaked in sweat. Then I heard his voice. After all these years the voice had not changed.

My words were hesitant and jerky. I had to take the initiative. "Ashraf."

He was silent for a while, as if trying to place the voice before saying calmly and with no hint of surprise, "Wafaa, how are you?"

I could see his smile in my mind's eye. It was warm, for one reason or another. He could hear my panting.

"Thanks for all the letters, Wafaa. I'm sorry, I wanted to write more, but I'm very busy these days."

I was quick to interrupt, tears welling up in my eyes. "It doesn't matter. Write when you want to, Ashraf. We missed you. All of us. I would like to talk to you about . . ."

He laughed for the first time. I felt as if he was enjoying talking to me, for some unknown reason.

"Wafaa, I'm proud of you, cousin. All these achievements!"

I almost fainted. "Really proud of me?" I whispered in a husky voice. The line was cut.

I shouted at the center's worker, "Please ring the number again!"

"Lines are busy," he said indifferently.

"Please," I whispered with tears in my eyes.

He looked at me with interest, for the first time. "He is your fiancé?"

"Yes," I said proudly.

He tried and tried, but in vain.

"Please," I whispered entreatingly.

He smiled suddenly, "My name is Sami. Come tomorrow. Try again."

The following day I went again. Sami rang Ashraf's number. I felt his smile as he heard my voice.

"I'm sorry. Yesterday the line was cut. Ashraf, am I delaying you with my calls? Can I phone you from time to time?" I asked shyly.

"Of course, Wafaa. But international calls are too expensive for you. Can I help you in any way?"

He had replied sharply, so I entreated, "Do you love me now? A little bit? You said you like me, remember?"

Was he suppressing a laugh? Was he? I could hear the tension in his voice. His words were disjointed. Somehow my words relieved the tension.

"You make me laugh, Wafaa. I had some trouble at work, but you made me laugh, as you used to do occasionally."

"Ashraf," I whispered with yearning.

"You are still behaving like an adolescent. Is that not true? Your mind has matured but not your heart."

"You have not answered my question."

"When I talk with you, I feel as though time has not moved on."

"You have not answered my question," I whispered joyfully.

"I don't remember the question."

I opened my mouth to say something. Then I felt he was just playing and kidding, as he used to do all the time. He loved to play, and he was using me as a toy, as a cat would play with a mouse before eating it or just discarding it when it got bored with the game. But I was happy.

"Do you have problems at work?" I asked empathetically.

I sensed his face frowning, as if his toy had been taken away;

"Yes. Problems. All of life is problems nowadays. 'Bye, Wafaa. I have to go back to work."

I didn't sleep that night. I had been saving most of what I earned in previous months. Rather than spending it on the needs and wants of the house, I decided to spend it on telephone calls to London.

Tomorrow I would phone him again. He said all of life was full of troubles. What troubles, Ashraf? Is it Lubna again? Had she returned to his life? Or was it a new woman hurting him? Was it his mother, and the death of his father? Maybe work problems? I wished I could have thrown myself into his arms, to feel his body shaking against my ribs. I wanted him—I wanted him as no woman ever wanted a man before.

Only God knew how much I wanted him. How much I resisted the urge and how I imagined myself submitting myself to him for nothing, without any regret. But I didn't do it.

After school and private lessons, I headed for the call center. The man knew me and knew the number by heart.

"You want to speak to your fiancé," he said indifferently. "I envy this fiancé of yours."

My embarrassment was evident. I felt ashamed of myself for lying. I asked for the number. When the voice came on it was tense.

"How are you, Wafaa?"

"I was worried about you. Are you okay, Ashraf?" I hastened to say.

"Thanks, Wafaa. 'Bye," he said tersely.

He hung up, leaving me stunned and frightened. How could he be so cruel?

The call center worker looked at me, smiling. "Is he being difficult or something?"

I made no reply. I walked a few steps, not knowing what to do. He had been tender with me before. He had given me hope for the future. Why was he playing games with me? Why me?

I would contact him once more to tell him off and to give him what he deserved. He was arrogant, treacherous, and depraved, and a million other things.

I had to contact him again. I would not go home this way. I just couldn't. So I returned to the call center.

The worker looked at me, smiling. "Same number?"

I nodded. I heard the bell ringing, and then his voice. My heart was pounding. "Ashraf, please don't hang up," I said automatically.

I felt he was smiling, but he said nothing.

"You know that you are my cousin, flesh and blood," I said.

"Yes, I know I am the son of your maternal aunt," he whispered. His voice was calmer.

"We are like brother and sister. Do you remember? You said before that we are like brother and sister."

"As I remember it, you didn't like what I said," he sighed.

"I like it. I never used to, but now I like it. I've changed. I have more self-confidence. I need no one. Do you see what I mean?" I said hopefully.

"No, I don't understand what you mean," he replied, finding my words amusing.

"I would like to be your friend and sister . . . sister only."

"You are my sister, Wafaa," he said automatically.

"Do not say that! Never!" I snapped.

I heard him chuckle. But he said nothing.

"I feel good when I talk to you. Can I talk to you now and then?" I said entreatingly.

"Of course you can. But I don't know about after you get married. Do you think your husband will accept this friendship?"

"I will never get married," I said decidedly, adding, "I will marry no one except you."

"Are we back to this nonsense, Wafaa?"

"I was just kidding. Of course I'll get married, but not now," I interrupted him.

He said nothing.

I asked suddenly, "What's wrong?"

"How did you known I'm not okay?" He asked astonished.

"From your voice. Didn't you say you're my flesh and blood?"

"I have problems, Wafaa." He said it casually.

The call center attendant warned me the line would be cut soon. Was he listening to the call then? It didn't matter. I gestured to him from the cabin shouting, "Please don't cut the line. Charge me for a second and a third call."

"Ashraf?"

No answer. Had the center's worker cut the line? Was Ashraf bored with me? Or was it just fate?

I didn't know.

My face was red. Tears were welling up in my eyes.

"Your fiancé?" the worker asked in a quiet, monotonous voice.

"Yes," I said without thinking.

"He must love you very much," he said in the same tone.

Was he mocking me? Or was that how he felt?

"He loves me very much." That's what the worker in the international call center said.

His words, even if sarcastic, were a comfort to me.

Ashraf didn't take my calls the following days, weeks, or months.

One morning I returned to the call center. I was extremely tense. During the previous days I had asked God to help me. Despair was eating me alive.

"There is no reply. No calls taken." He smiled as I looked at him in despair.

I was heading for the door when he said, "Do you want to try again?"

"Yes, please." I smiled. My eyes were bright with hope. Our eyes met.

"I will try, but I have a condition," he said quickly.

I looked at him accusingly.

"What is your name?"

"Wafaa." I was getting impatient.

"I will try, Miss Wafaa, because you are very good-hearted. But I have one condition."

"What?" I said sharply.

"You ask your fiancé to find a job for me in London."

I smiled innocently. I had expected something else. But I liked Sami. For a few seconds I felt we were alike. Each of us was looking for the impossible. I needed a friend. I feared all men. I thought of no one except Ashraf.

"I promise you," I said with zeal.

"Will you come again tomorrow?" He was smiling.

"I will try tomorrow," I said energetically.

The following morning I felt extremely lonely. I felt the black hole within me growing every day.

When he saw me, he smiled. "Cabin five. I will phone the number for you."

I waited in anticipation and anxiety.

Then a voice came. It was not Ashraf's; it was Sami's. "There is no reply."

"Try again," I whispered, imploring him.

"There is no answer, Wafaa."

I came out of the cabin looking tense.

"He may be away. Try tomorrow."

I tried the following day and days.

One day the center was full of people. Tears were welling up in my eyes. Sami's eyes never left mine.

"Is he really your fiancé?" he asked, looking at me closely.

"What do you mean?" I snapped with tears flowing.

"You are like a sister to me," he said shyly.

I eyed him with surprise. This "you are like a sister to me" seemed written all over my forehead. But Sami was different. I could see something different in his eyes. It might be infatuation.

He hastened to add, "Take it easy, Wafaa."

"Don't utter my name, if you don't mind. I don't know you."

"I'm sorry." He was embarrassed.

I headed for the door. He followed me, asking, "Where to?"

"My home."

"Where is that?"

"It's none of your business, if you don't mind," I said, looking at him in surprise and wiping my tears.

After a short pause I whispered, "Thanks, Sami, for trying that number for me. Will you try again tomorrow?"

"I will try it every day, for your sake. Did I not say you are like a sister to me?"

"Don't say a thing. I want to hear nothing. Starting tomorrow, I will go to a different call center."

"Have I bothered you that much? I'm sorry. Do you fear me, or fear your feelings?"

I opened my eyes wide in surprise. His eyelids were fluttering nervously, as if he were about to confess his love to me.

Then he said, "Of course, I'm not like him. I don't live in London, and I don't get paid in sterling, but my father is a butcher."

I said nothing. So he continued, encouraged, "He's not your fiancé?"

I looked around me. I was on platform three waiting for the Damanhour train. Sami was talking nonstop, but I heard nothing. I was not afraid of him. I saw only one dream, and one man. My blood curdled when I imagined myself with a different man. But I had no fear of Sami; he was peaceful and simple. He wanted to travel to Britain or Saudi Arabia or to get married and settle in Egypt. He was different from me. He was more flexible, and more optimistic. I envied him. He had seen my weakness.

I looked at him suddenly without hearing a word of what he was saying.

"God be with you, Wafaa," he said quickly.

He left quietly. Everything he did was quiet and tender. He was an idealist. I liked him, and I sensed that he would make a good husband who would try his best to make his wife happy, in every gentle way. But who would listen to reason? Not me. I heard no voice except that of my imagination. He understood that hope was impossible. He was quick-thinking but simple. He didn't like playing games. I was like a mouse waiting to deliver itself as a sacrifice to a waiting cat.

And I came to know how sacrifices were offered.

I returned home, determined to stop talking to Ashraf. Instead, I decided to send him another letter telling him about Sami. Maybe he'd feel jealous . . . but he wouldn't do that, would he?

I said a lot of prayers. I was talking to God everywhere, all the time. Time, place, and form never bothered me. My relationship with God was strong. Talking to him made me feel comfortable and at ease. I stopped going to the international call center. I reminded myself that I would live whether Ashraf came back or not. I might not get married, but I would live.

~

The dream seemed far-fetched but attainable, occasionally. I wrote to him once more.

Ashraf,

What's wrong with you? Is it a woman who has entered your life and confused you? Has your father's death affected you this much? Do you miss Egypt? Are you afraid? Talk to me, open up, and tell me everything. How I wish I could help you.

I had no idea whether people around me knew that I phoned and wrote to him from time to time. Nor did I know whether they thought I was crazy or not. I had no close contact with those around me. I used to ask about Sally now and then. I loved her baby son. I would tell him some of my fantasies and tell him stories. My relationship with Kareem was not close; he was a loner. As for Mother and Father, I never felt that they were close to me. My feelings toward them had not changed much, but I started to feel a certain warmth and affection toward them as they got older. I was more tender toward Mother as I saw her changing with the passage of time.

I would return home from work extremely exhausted, close the door of my room, and write letters to Ashraf. My love for him was a full-time job.

Two months later, I received a letter from Ashraf. I could see the day of his return to me getting nearer and nearer.

That day's letter seemed heavy and thick. I grasped it eagerly as I walked quickly by the seaside. I sat on the wooden bench in front of the high waves. I took a deep breath, pulled out a cheese sandwich, and began eating as I opened the letter. I put the sandwich away and held the paper with both hands as if it were a baby needing protection, a source of pride.

Wafaa,

A catastrophe struck me. Everything is lost. A year's work vanished in moments. May God destroy the home of the Conservative Party. A curse upon it, and upon its times.

Everything I ever owned is gone.

It does not matter. I have to save myself; otherwise, I will spend the rest of my youth in jail. I can't explain to you, and I don't want to—nor do I have the time. I feel a strong urge to throw up—forgive me. I am going to stop writing now.

(The rest is written in pencil, not in the Parker fountain pen that he usually preferred.)

I had bought three houses on installments guaranteed by my job. I entered and got clients into financial deals that all recorded great losses. Housing prices dropped sharply, and the interest rate went crazy. I am under threat of seven years in jail, Wafaa.

I took a risk. Everyone does it. Everyone else wins and becomes rich. As for me, I don't know what to do. I have to move fast. I hate writing letters. I may not write to you again.

I think I have to migrate. Mother does not stop crying, and she does not believe what has happened. I think I have to migrate. Britain is no longer my home. I will move to Spain or maybe to America. Everyone wants to migrate to America, as it is the country of the drowning and the desperate. I will move to America. Not bad. I will start again.

The problem was not my mental abilities. The problem was that of a shaky economy in a country fluctuating between tradition and greed . . . etc., but I don't know.

I hate poverty, and I fear it. I fear it more than anything else. I wish my death now, or my paralysis, rather than lose all my assets in bad deals. It was a national crisis that hit the whole country. To be struck with paralysis is better than serving others for peanuts.

I hate poverty, Wafaa.

I told no one before, but I despise the poor. Now I have become one of them.

It doesn't matter.

I took my two passports, the Egyptian and the British. I gazed at both of them. I have to dispose of my British passport now. I fear jail. I shredded my British passport like I was tearing up pieces of my British identity altogether.

Every age has its own passport.

I will travel using the Egyptian one. I got my visa, and I will go to the land of dreams and illusions. Pray for me, Wafaa. I know you to be religious. Are you still religious?

I have small funds in an American bank. I transferred some of my own money and other people's to that account. What do you expect? Go hungry? I will get the money and start anew. Why do I tell you all this when in fact you mean nothing to me? Maybe that is exactly the reason: that you are someone who means nothing to me—even if I strip naked before you, it would mean nothing to me as well.

~

I reread the letter many times. I didn't finish my cheese sandwich. He might never write to me again. I might never set eyes on him again. He might even commit suicide.

This was crazy. Of course I would never see him again. Why would I not hold fast to an impossible dream like other Egyptians or like all other human beings? Who among us would not hold fast to an impossible dream?

I went home and asked Mother about my aunt and her son, and their news. She said Aunt would come to visit in a couple of weeks, but she said nothing about Ashraf. A week passed, and Mother found out that Ashraf was going through some serious financial problems and that he had left the country. She knew no more.

I didn't write another letter to him for weeks. I was afraid that if I wrote to him about how much I loved him, he would fear me and stop writing. I was afraid and confused. When we traveled to Cairo to meet Ashraf's mother at the airport, we stayed the night with my paternal aunt Aliyya, like we used to. My heart ached because of my fear and longing for him, and because of the despair that was gripping me once more.

My aunt crouched on the sofa, which was upholstered in pink, where she loved to sit and hold court, issuing instructions, making decisions, and seeing them carried out.

I was extremely tense. Mother was in a state of alert for what my aunt might say. Kareem was getting ready to give his fatwa edicts in all matters, being a student in the faculty of commerce. As for Sally, she started shouting at her baby son like he was her obstacle to eternal happiness.

My aunt sucked air through her teeth and said to Mother, "I heard that Ashraf, your nephew, flew from Britain. He embezzled money from the bank where he worked."

Mother looked at her contemptuously and said aggressively, "Those are envious rumors."

My aunt said calmly, "Manaal, your nephew deserved the worst from God for his drinking and womanizing and other mischief."

Mother was about to speak, but Kareem stated knowingly, "I knew this would happen. Mother, you don't know about the economic problems in Britain. Everyone is suffering because of the bad policies of the Conservative Party."

My aunt said dryly, "Problems in Britain! And what do you call what we have here?"

Kareem rejoined, while Mother watched him with admiration, "I advised Ashraf to remain in Egypt and start a project with me. It seemed that he thought we were after his money. This is the fate of those who do not trust their own."

Mother said dryly, "This is the result of the evil eye."

"What can he be envied for? I don't envy him. I have a son. May God protect my son, who, unlike Ashraf, is neither a thief nor corrupt," Aunt Aliyya said, displeased.

I swallowed my saliva in pain and said nothing. Mother screamed and shouted and got ready to leave my aunt's house. Sally tried to calm her down. Matters ended with Mother taking a small room in Aunt's house while my aunt complained to Sally about Mother's excessive sensitivity and about how tired she was after having cooked all that fish just for her. I began to feel a strong urge to look for my old friend, the blunt knife. I did not.

I just closed my eyes, bit my lip, and began writing once more: *Please, Ashraf, tell me your news. If you don't, I won't die, but I will be very sad indeed. You are good-hearted, Ashraf. I know it. You deserve the best.*

I wanted to send the letter right away, but I remembered I didn't have his address. I didn't know where to send the letter. I felt lost, but I didn't resort to the blunt knife. I just found myself mumbling, "God is merciful."

The arrival of Ashraf's mother from Britain calmed me. I knew she would tell us all his news.

I was at the Cairo Airport waiting hopefully for her arrival, five years after Ashraf's departure. Five years during which Ashraf lost his father and all that he owned in a matter of just moments. Five years during which I thought about nothing except him, while our lives turned upside down. All of us. If only he would come now with Aunt. If only he would come to marry me. If only.

Grief was registered on Aunt's face. She had been wearing black despite the passage of two years since the death of her husband. In the car I sat beside her.

"How is he doing, Aunt Laila?" I whispered.

"He is with God, who will look after him," she said coldly.

My heart almost stopped. I asked her in a hoarse voice, "Who?"

"The deceased. May God rest his soul."

I sighed, completely relieved, and asked, "How is Ashraf?"

"In America," she said, somewhat indifferently.

"Do you have his address?"

"No, but he contacted me. He's fine. Many friends advise me to take off my black dress, but I can't. It was a lifetime companionship, Wafaa."

I couldn't understand my aunt. Had she lost her mind? Why was she trying to deceive us? We all knew Mahmoud, her late husband, and we all knew her past relationship with him. However, what puzzled me more was her avoidance of the subject of Ashraf.

She was ashamed of the collapse of her son's fortunes. Or was the matter too much for her? Maybe both. She used to smile proudly, with bright, shining eyes whenever his name was mentioned. Her eyes still shone whenever the name was mentioned, but there were no smiles anymore. Instead, she would just lower her head and say nothing.

There was a lot I failed to understand about the conduct of those around me. It seemed to me that my aunt was no longer living on the existence of Ashraf but on the made-up memory of her late husband. It seemed to me also that imagination began to control our lives, and that the dream had become preferable to reality.

My aunt, who had cried her eyes out over the death of the Egyptian idol singer Abdalhaleem Haafiz, didn't seem like an Egyptian anymore. She had no desire to stay in Egypt, except as a tourist. She returned after staying for only two weeks in order to catch up with friends, the cold weather, and the National Health Service.

As for myself, I used to go to work in the morning and do my private tutoring in the evening. I was teaching the history of the Arab world and of Egypt at the high school level. I used to give a lot of private sessions. I would prompt pupils on the six principles of the Egyptian revolution, the three things "eradicated" and the three things that were established every day, twenty-five times a day:

Eradication of colonialism,

Eradication of corruption and control of capital,
Eradication of the king and his allies,
Establishing a proper democratic life,
Establishing social justice,
Establishing a strong national army.

ᴖ

I needed work to forget. I still loved him and dreamed of him.
Three months later he wrote to me. Yes, he wrote again.

On my arrival in America, I was waiting eagerly for the morning to go to the bank to withdraw my funds. It is rather funny, you
know, for I forgot the password for my account. So when I went
to the bank in the morning with my Egyptian passport—I had to
destroy my British passport, as I had told you, or I would not have
been able to leave the country—I zealously presented the passport
to the cashier, and she shook her head and said, "But the holder of
the account is British."

"Yes. I have two passports: Egyptian and British."

"We need the British passport."

"I don't have it."

"We can't let you have this money, except on the identity of
the passport with which you deposited the funds."

I was not used to losing my cool, but I did. I was shaking from
head to toe. So I shouted at the cashier and the bank manager,
and shook the cashier's shoulder shouting, "My money! I want my
money!"

She just repeated, "You have no money here."

"My money!"

"You have no money here. An Egyptian passport and no
account number! The holder of the account is British."

I spent the night at a police station. Over the following two
days, I tried again. I hoped to God that I would remember the
number. 3519? 3591? Or maybe 3951? I could not.

This is the end of the story of Ashraf the happy Briton.

I believe everyone should have a bath, daily. This was what I
believed before lodging in the poor housing project in Virginia.

That is what I call it. It is the abode of the tortured. The poor of Egypt have a lot of wit and sense of humor. The poor of America are submerged in humiliation.

I could not even pass water, Wafaa. Do you know this feeling of urine being detained inside your body like words stick in your throat? I feel a strong wish to be dead. I had always thought I was strong and clever.

You know, Wafaa, I feel a strange weakness as I look at my neighbors in the same hostel, indeed the same toilet. Where we live is not a house; it is a huge toilet. The smell of filth is everywhere, especially the kitchen and the bathroom. The latter is always full of tissue paper soaked in urine, vomit, and shit. The kitchen is stuffed with cheap liquor, stale potato chips, and rotten pasta covered in tomato sauce.

I can no longer enter the bathroom or the kitchen. I just can't. I have no money now. Mother will send me some, she said, but not now. Hope is what I live for. Poverty is not for me.

Jack, a neighbor of mine, is in his early sixties. I pity him a lot, Wafaa. I think he is unemployed now. He does not bathe, Wafaa. He just sits listening to the radio for hours every day, dressed in his striped trousers, shabby shirt, and heavy coat, which carries different odors and smells. I do not intend to describe those to you now.

As for Pedro, the Mexican, he is a fugitive like me, maybe. I don't know. He came to America to work, which I think he is doing. Every day he came in drunk. Most times he would vomit, and wait for his girlfriend to turn up to spend the night with him. The screams and the quarreling! You can't tell who is beating whom. Then they fall silent, almost.

I am beginning to hate alcohol, Wafaa. I used to enjoy champagne and white wine with pistachios. Now I cannot tolerate the smell of beer, or vomit, Pedro or Jack.

What is to be done now?

I work in a fried chicken place. So I hate the smell of fried chicken, too. When Mother sends me some money, I will eat anything except fried chicken. I locked up my brain, Wafaa. It is not functioning anymore. I no longer eat regularly. I can't. Today I looked at my reflection in the mirror; it was the face of a man I never laid eyes on before. Gray hair is taking over my head. My face looks bony.

I couldn't believe the contents of the letter. The events he described seemed to me like a silly play performed by Ashraf, or a game. I know he adores games. I couldn't understand what he said, and I didn't believe it. I inspected the letter. I found his address; he was in America, in Virginia, as I believed. He was not lying. It was difficult for me to imagine him in such surroundings. I couldn't judge him as my aunt and mother did. It was difficult for me to understand why Aunt had not helped him. She may have tried; I don't know. She may have been saving her money for a rainy day. After giving it a lot of thought, it occurred to me that Aunt might not have had a lot of money. She might have been involved in her son's deals. The picture became crystal clear to me: Ashraf had worked in a bank. He had speculated in the stock exchange using his money, his inheritance from his father, his mother's, as well as his clients'. He loved speculating. Because of the banking crisis, he'd collapsed, together with his clients. As he was not prudent, his bank had lost a lot as well. So the young financial expert millionaire, the clever, good-looking one, ended with a sentence of seven years in jail.

The truth revealed itself to me slowly, through bits from his letters, news, his mother, and my imagination. Why hadn't his mother helped him? Because she could not. She had no money to spare. Also, she couldn't contact him for fear that the British police would track him down.

Events seemed unreal, as if they were happening to other people. Disasters used to be other people's domain. Now they fell on my sweetheart as if they had always been linked to him. I had never thought even for a few moments that Ashraf had made a mistake, even if he had no intention of hurting others, even if he deliberately smuggled his money and other people's money into America so that he would not live like a pauper. I could not think along these lines. Anyone who saw Ashraf ended up sympathizing with him. He just loved to play.

∾

I went to my private tutoring classes. Then I took the train, second class, as I do every day. I sat on the blue leather seat and heard a monotonous voice asking me for my ticket. I gave him my travel card. Then I closed my eyes to dream. Was there a woman who would find and rescue him? Was he in contact with Lubna?

I knew for sure he wasn't. What was she doing now? Had she forgotten him? Would she reconcile with herself and with him after knowing what had become of him?

I was preoccupied with Lubna, and with my sister as well. I was worried for her and angry with her at the same time. I couldn't understand how everyone could have known about her secret marriage, and yet none of them had raised any objection. Even Father hadn't objected. Well, he had initially, but her husband had offered her security. Also, marriage was the public announcement of the relationship. Everyone knew (except for his wife and children, or so he thought). I hated my sister's deceptions, her ruthlessness, and her way of living. As for me, I refused to get married. I was twenty-six years old and still refused to marry.

~

My sister sat, sighing, as she plucked her eyebrows nervously, and said to Mother, "She is jealous of me! This wife of his! She is an ugly woman in every way. She knows that he doesn't want her. Nevertheless, she is holding fast to him and to his failed children."

Mother said, moved and affected, "Poor you! What luck!"

"She hates me, Mother. She hates me because he loves me so much. My wretched luck put her in my way. If only she would die! If only she would go to hell!"

I winced as I saw the cruelty in Sally's eyes.

"Sally," I whispered.

She didn't look at me, but she followed her son with her eyes as he ate a piece of pizza, covering his face with the sauce. Then she rose and smacked him on his hand as she carried the plate to the kitchen.

"A dumb, stupid boy! I gave birth to an idiot. Oh damn you! Damn you!" she shouted.

Mother rose to calm the child.

"You need a break, love. I'll take the baby with me today."

I looked in pain as I dreamed about a new letter from Ashraf.

"Sally, what harm has your son done?" I whispered.

"And me, what harm have I done, Wafaa? Everyone is against me; no one cares for me."

"But you think only of yourself," I intervened sharply.

Her eyes were bathed in tears. "But you didn't lose your husband less than two years after marrying him. You don't know what deprivation means. You don't know the meaning of widowhood. You don't know the suffering I've gone through. Why did I become a mother? Just my bad luck."

"It is God's will, Sally," I said tenderly.

"Then don't interfere," she said decidedly.

I shook my head in despair, grabbed my purse, and headed for the door.

She called after me, "Don't be angry with me, Wafaa. It's his first wife in my mind all the time. She incites him against me. She hates me."

"Of course she hates you! What do you expect? She's also a victim," I said as I sat once more.

"No, she deserves all that. Her heart is dark, and her intentions are ugly and evil," she asserted.

"Is that your opinion or his?" I asked sarcastically.

"Our opinion," she boasted.

The following day, my nephew moved in with us so that my sister could dedicate herself to her husband and his other wife.

I remembered my sister when her husband died. She was holding herself together all the time, accepting condolences calmly. A few days later, I saw her squatting on the floor in the dark, crying her eyes out in a way I had never seen her do before. I hugged her and whispered, "It's all right, sister. It's all right. He is now relieved and comfortable."

"He is relieved and comfortable. True, of course, but what about me?" she said bitterly.

From that day on she avoided mentioning his name. She never cried again. I don't know whether she envied him for being dead or was angry with him, pitying herself, or was just determined to have a life once more.

That day, while I was making tea for Mother and for her, Sally came over to me and said with mischief, "Why do you refuse marriage? Still in love with Ashraf?"

Her question was a surprise to me, so all I said was, "Me?"

She interrupted me as she rubbed some cream on her hands, "Cairo weather dries the hands. You know, Wafaa, everyone knows of your love for Ashraf. We all know, Wafaa." She paused then added, "Ashraf is a handsome man, but he left years ago. Haven't you noticed?"

"Ashraf's gone, I know that," I said as my hand trembled.

"No, you don't. You haven't noticed," she said as she stretched out on the chair and rubbed the cream on her arms. "What are you waiting for? Aunt Aliyya has a suitor—a doctor—for you. You are now in your late twenties, and time is flying."

"I want no groom from Aunt Aliyya," I snapped.

"Don't worry—he's respectable. I saw him. Wafaa, please, just meet him. Don't disappoint your parents like this for the sake of a man who departed ten years ago," she said through her giggles.

"I don't think about Ashraf. I haven't thought about him since he left," I asserted.

"Well, then, you will meet the doctor," she dared me.

"I will not," I replied mechanically.

Not long after, my younger sister took responsibility for me, inviting Aunt Aliyya and the future groom to her house. I found myself sitting on the gold-colored sofa in the living room, in my sister's house. I saw the groom-to-be, sitting uncomfortably; I didn't look directly at him. I saw my aunt with pride radiating from her face, and my sister showing off her new china tea set. The surprise didn't stun me; it just reminded me that my true love was far, far away.

Aunt started her introduction strongly: "Wafaa, God protects her; she is religious. She works in a girls' school. But, naturally, she will quit her job after marriage. Isn't that right, Wafaa?"

"No, I will never quit my job."

Embarrassed, my sister said to the future groom, "What are your future plans, Doctor?"

"I will go to the Gulf, naturally. This country has become very difficult," he said calmly. Then addressing me, "What do you think? Life in Egypt has become difficult, hasn't it?"

"Yes. Difficult. The hegemony of capital makes life difficult everywhere. I do not object to rich people being here, but the poor should have a right to rich people's fortunes," I said with confidence.

"Wafaa is an educated girl. She is also a good cook. She has never been with anyone before. She's from a good family," my aunt boasted.

I looked at her. I had no idea why she was doing this. I also viewed her as an enemy of Ashraf, an enemy he didn't even know. I didn't know whether she hated him that much or just loved me, or if she merely wanted to impose her control on all members of the family.

I wished the evening would end soon. The groom-to-be began talking to me.

I looked at him, shuddering. How could I submit my body to him when he was not Ashraf? I couldn't give myself to this man.

"You are from Damanhour, of course. Behaira Province people are the best." He was smiling calmly.

"I don't know." I was terse.

He must have thought that I was just shy, so he continued, "If matters work out, God willing, you will be very happy in the Gulf. Life is easy, and everything is abundant, even Egyptian food. I love Jew's mallow a lot—the fresh one, mind you. As for the frozen one . . ."

"The frozen one is no good. Wafaa cooks a splendid Jew's mallow," my aunt interrupted zealously.

"I don't have time for cooking anymore," I said dryly.

The echo of Ashraf's voice came to me: "One day I will cook for you."

How could that man compare to the magic and tenderness of Ashraf? I might not have liked Ashraf's tenderness back when I constructed him from my imagination. But I loved him whether tender, violent, or cruel. I could not tolerate the cruelty, or the tenderness of people other than him.

And what could this man offer me?

Maybe a quiet life, maybe a boring life where I would become a wife, thinking about how to cook Jew's mallow and how to save money on the household budget, and how to make my husband happy.

I would have accepted such a life from Ashraf. But Ashraf was not like this man. Ashraf would have given me the expertise of pistachio sellers. He would have quenched my thirst with drinks from different places.

Ashraf would have opened Aladdin's cave to me. How much I missed him!

When the groom-to-be left, I felt hugely relieved. But my younger sister suddenly exploded. "What is this silly nonsense you said about work and poverty?"

I looked at her angrily. She had never been my friend. I had been cruel to her in the past, and it was time for her to be cruel to me now. My aunt looked keenly at me, apprehensively. They were all expecting my reply.

"I don't want to get married, Sally," I said calmly. "You know that."

"She wants to work, and earn her keep. She loves the bother," my sister said as she smiled at my aunt.

"And you! Why don't you work? Why? Mother is looking after your son. What do you do all day? Nothing. You just wait for the husband to arrive. Nothing else. It's not enough, Sally. You're clever. You have your high school diploma. Believe me, do something for yourself," I said energetically and truthfully.

She was angry to hear me say that in front of Aunt, but she restrained herself. "I need no job. Praise to God, my husband is sufficient. And he doesn't want me to work."

"Why? It's selfish of him. Isn't it enough that you have to wait for him for two or three days every time he visits?"

"I wait for him for two or three days, rather than waiting for a man who doesn't want me, and who never turns up. You understand me, Wafaa? A man who never loved me at all, a man who may have married now once, twice, or three times," she said firmly.

I said nothing. Her reply was severe and was delivered before Aunt Aliyya.

I felt my face get hot, as if I had a sudden fever.

My aunt looked at me, stunned.

"Ashraf? Are you waiting for Ashraf?"

"That's a lie," I said in a hoarse voice

"The devil played tricks on you, girl. He is irresponsible and decadent. Wise up, Wafaa," Aunt said half-crying.

"You always accuse him of being irresponsible and decadent, as if those accusations are capable of making me hate him. I don't believe he is irresponsible or decadent. He might have been brought up in a different country, in a different way. But he's not decadent," I said aggressively.

"You don't hate him? You love him, then?"

"Yes, I love him. I love him and wish to marry him. He doesn't want me. Had he wanted me, I would have been with him wherever he is," I said in despair, with tears filling my eyes.

My aunt covered her mouth, perplexed, and said, "You deserve death. It's true that burying girls alive was a blessing. I wish your father had killed you before . . ."

My sister interrupted her, "Aunt, her nerves are stretched. She doesn't love him. Wafaa is a reasonable girl. I'll talk to her."

"I love him. Why do I have to defend myself? What's wrong with that? I love him!" I persisted.

"Enough of that, Wafaa. What if she tells Father?" my sister declared.

"What will she say? That his crazy daughter loves a man who left years ago, and who never felt the same about her? Will Father object to my impossible love for Ashraf, when he didn't object to your common-law marriage to an already married man?"

My sister burst into tears and said with bitterness, "All this cruelty, Wafaa. All your lies. You have always been jealous of me. Why?"

My aunt interrupted contemptuously, "No sense of shame, and no manners. May God curse all girls and their offspring. You are a disgrace to the family, Wafaa."

She rose, getting ready to leave.

"Please wait, Aunt," Sally said hopefully.

"It's all right, darling. You have done nothing wrong. Men have the right to marry one, or two. Your husband is a respectable man. The condition for proper marriage is to make it public. We all know that you are married to him, keeping it a secret so his other wife knows nothing about it," she told Sally, patting her on the shoulder.

She then looked at me and added dryly to Sally, "Your husband is not a thief. He is not fleeing from justice or from anything else."

When she finally rose again, she took her purse, kissed Sally, and said to her, "May God be with you, daughter."

I felt a great relief. I wiped my tears and said, "Are you pleased, Sally? Everyone knows that I love him."

"You are stupid. If Aunt told Father and all our relatives, your name will be in the mouths of everyone. Why, Wafaa?" Sally said in despair.

"It's my fault, then. Excuse me, Sally, I have work to do," I said coldly, and added before opening the door, "I'm not jealous of you, Sally. Not now. In the past, yes, I was. But not now."

She did not comment.

I have no idea whether or not Aunt told Father. He never mentioned it. He never spoke about the suitor. I never wondered whether he knew. What I knew was that for one reason or another he respected me. I don't know if my name was on everyone's tongue. I had no time to worry about that. I was busy with work and with him.

A few days later I made up with my sister, as we usually did after we had torn each other to pieces. We used to do that a lot. I was waiting for a letter from him.

His letters were rare and discontinuous but sincere. It was as if he poured his heart out on a few pages or just a single short page. So I started writing to him sincerely and briefly.

Ashraf,

Do not lose hope. Why don't you return to Egypt? Egypt is your country. Come for my sake and for your own sake. I miss you. I miss seeing your face, although it has never left my mind. As I have overcome grief and desperation, so will you. You are the hope. All the hope. You are everything. So come back to Egypt, Ashraf. I know that you did not grow up in Egypt, but you are Egyptian. Your features and your speech are all Egyptian. Nothing to worry about. Look after yourself. I still love you.

I had to remind him of my feelings. He might return.

What baffled me in his letters was that he mostly ignored my words. He said that he wanted to write as if he were writing to a stranger. He just poured out his feelings. I began to think I was nothing to him. However, he always referred to me by name, as "Wafaa." So he knew who I was. He knew me well. In fact, he knew the most intimate things about me. He knew my vulnerability and madness. That might have encouraged him to pour out his feelings.

⌖

He wrote to me again.

I was sitting on the old fence in front of the house where I am living with my disgusting neighbors. I was there to catch my breath and for another reason:

I hate the stench of sweat, alcohol, and rotten burnt tomatoes that reigns over the house. I looked at the graffiti on the old wall—words, letters, and drawings of hearts in red and blue.

I felt a hand touching my shoulder. I turned. It was Pedro's girlfriend. I don't know where she comes from. She may be of an eastern European origin. She is very skinny. Her blonde hair flows down her back. She kept her hand on my shoulder and whispered, "You do not hit women, do you?"

"I beg your pardon?"

"He beats me. You probably hear him beating me every night," she whispered, half-crying.

I looked at her, stunned. Then I realized what she wanted. I was craving a woman. I was not used to wanting women. She came nearer to me. She smelled strongly of alcohol. I do not remember what happened afterwards. But I felt disgusted by her. Do you believe me, Wafaa? No, I will not sink so low as to kiss or touch a woman like that after all the high-class girls of Britain and after my love for Lubna.

Only a few minutes later, Pedro came out of the house and went after me with his fists. It was the first time ever for me to hit a man that hard, and I feel good and proud about it. Pedro was bleeding after my blows. I wiped drops of blood from my nose. I walked down the street that was lined with miserable houses and littered with loud noises, drugs, and prostitutes.

I never felt such satisfaction before. But I soon hated myself and felt disgusted with everything. When will Mother's money arrive? I have not brought even my certificates with me; how I hate poverty, Wafaa. It was like Kassim, brother of Ali Baba, forgetting the code word. But Kassim was greedy. I merely want to live as I used to.

～

I imagined Ashraf sitting on the old wall making love to the eastern European girl. I could see despair and disgust in his eyes. I was somewhat jealous. I pitied him and wished he would give me the chance to love him, as I wanted.

I wrote:

> Ashraf? Have you made love to her? Do not lie to me. I know you well. You cannot do that to the girlfriend of another man, even if he was in the habit of abusing her, and even if she offered herself to you. Tell the truth. Are you still in touch with her? I am just asking because you are flesh and blood.

I waited for the reply. I regretted the words I had used. They were rash and stupid.

So I wrote once more:

> Don't be angry with me. You have the right to love and live, but you need someone who appreciates you and loves you deeply.
> Love, Wafaa.

I sent him the above brief letter. Two weeks later, his reply came.

> Wafaa,
> I am not angry with you. I can't be. You are part of my flesh and blood, as you say. And what else? You are like a sister to me. My sister does not speak about these things, shameful Wafaa. You are a well-brought-up girl. Or have you changed?

I could see him laughing as he wrote his letter. It was a warm letter.

My life went on, revolving around his brief letters. I visited my sister before receiving his last letter. I carried on with my teaching. I sent him two letters to which he made no replies. In the first one I begged him to return to Egypt:

> Ashraf,
> Please, Ashraf, why are you exposing yourself to humiliation in the country of Westerners? Return to me and to Egypt. Please, I love you. Even if we do not become rich, it is enough for me to live with you. I will make you happy and wait on you throughout the

night. You will not be exposed to any humiliation. Please, Ashraf.
I love you.

I wrote a longer letter saying the same things. He didn't reply. He
probably thought I was silly and what I said was just rubbish: I love you,
come back to me . . . for better, for worse . . . return to your country, and
so forth.

He must have smiled sarcastically as he read my letter. He might even
have hated me—that is, if he ever loved me at all.

A whole month passed, and he didn't write. Then another month
passed. I started to worry. So I wrote to him, once more.

*Did I say anything that made you angry? Don't stop writing to me. If
you do . . .* I thought briefly. He doesn't like threats, so I continued, *Talk to
me. Are we not friends? When you have time, write to me. No, write now. I
have no patience left.*

I was furious with myself for my silly words.

I sent him news about my sister, Mother, Kareem, and the neighbors.
I wrote to him about everyone except me and him.

Mother insisted that I get married. She often exploded in rage: "Stop
this crazy business! What are you dreaming about? No one knows his
whereabouts."

I used to ignore her comments, calmly, without trying to convince
her. I would talk to her about any subject except the subject of my
marriage.

I was extremely jealous of Lubna, for he had touched her and
embraced her, but I wouldn't envy any other girl he got to know. I felt
nothing but pride when he told me about the eastern European girl,
Pedro's girlfriend. That meant he trusted me. I must have been someone
close to him to some extent. The small intimate details that surfaced in
his letters fed me for days upon days. They would be my strength, sanctu-
ary, and guardian.

Then he wrote:

Sometimes one thinks he has finished once and for all with
certain people. You know what I mean? Take Lubna, for instance.

She never left my mind at all. Lubna, who disowned me and my riches for the sake of her convictions and belief in a cause that I did not comprehend.

She never thought, even for a second, that her cause and convictions might not have any value. During the last few days I have felt a strange sensation of craving and a sense of relief that I have not experienced for some time.

I went to California to attend a conference about the politics and economies of the Middle East. In fact, there was no reason for going there. I just longed to see the rich and the intellectuals. I felt a yearning for the life that I have lost forever, and that I occasionally feel will never return.

I was driving my small car to California feeling a strange dullness. My brain felt as if it was being eaten by an old spider that laced it with sugar before eating it slowly. Then I felt a loathing for myself that I have never felt before, even while I lived in the filthy house with Pedro and Jack.

What makes me go to this conference? In what capacity? I have no interest in the economy of the Middle East or its problems. I am concerned with nothing, except my extreme self-loathing. I know what you'll say: that I should not despise myself because you are in love with me.

I am laughing at you now, Wafaa, at your naïveté, and madness. What do you expect, and what do you want? I don't know anymore. But never mind. Let's talk about something else. I borrowed one hundred dollars. I had five hundred dollars in savings. I spent it all to go and stay two days in a hotel. Two days only, to feel rich again. The maid would come every day in the morning to change the linen and the towels that I would have thrown on the floor. I would stretch out on my bed while she picked them up off the floor and replaced them with fresh ones. I would just sigh and watch the satellite TV station.

Water flooding strongly from the shower hit my head and covered my body, and I would feel an unprecedented happiness. What was I saying . . . Ah . . . yes, Wafaa. I was walking around the conference hall. All around the place was full of suits, caviar, and the elegance of the conference.

I decided to spend my annual vacation at a California conference every year. Two days merely, during which I feel all the glory and the pride.

What do I own now? Incidentally, my mother will visit me this year. When I get my American passport I will become more confident and free. The case with the bank and the real estate will be over, once and for all. I will then be a new American man. I may even get back my money.

Well, what was I saying?

I sat listening to the speeches and presentations and looking at the elegant clothes and the luxury cars, and at all those Europeans, Americans, and Japanese who are interested in the problems of the Middle East. But why? And what is the Middle East anyway? Turkey, Iran, Israel, Egypt, and the Arab world? An odd group in a narrow spot, joined only by their miserable luck and ancient geography as well as their leaders, the decision makers, naturally.

I closed me eyes and heard someone speaking in bad but clear English, and it was her! I am talking about Lubna, who rejected and wounded me. I saw her, Wafaa. I met her at the conference.

A fit of laughter seized me. I had to leave the hall. Did she see me? Maybe. I did not laugh because I saw her. I laughed because she was talking about the economy, and the development and democracy of the Middle East. Lubna Thaabit, whom I had loved, and whom I never took seriously, nor believed a word of what she said.

In the conference she talked about democracy in America. Lubna, the communist who had suffered jail, who disowned me and refused to stay with me in a five-star hotel, and who rejected a gold necklace and a diamond ring . . . and who rejected me!

I am not crazy, Wafaa, but I saw her today. Yes. I was moved. My heart was beating fast. But I kept my cool and sat in the splendid lobby of the hotel, expecting her to come anytime. She did come. I knew she would. My feelings toward her are conflicted:

fury, yearning, and coldness. It had been ten years since I last saw her. Has she changed? Yes, she has. Her jet-black hair has become red. Her facial bones became more prominent, and she seemed thinner. The face carried more wrinkles. She still wore her jeans. She tied her ponytail hair as she always did. She still moved her hands in every direction nervously. I saw all that in seconds. Lubna was the same Lubna who used to embrace me tightly and scream, "I love you, you feudalist exploiter of the poor!"

I smiled to myself, recollecting the first pair of shoes that Mother bought me when I started school. The shoes were shining like Father's. That was the past. A past that has finished. We have to forget the past, Wafaa. Understand? Forget, Wafaa. Do not hang on to rotten ropes. There was nothing between us. Do you remember? I don't know why I write to you at all. Maybe I have to stop it. I will not write to you after this. But you would like to know what happened between me and Lubna. I want to tell you about what occurred, Wafaa. I don't know. I have to tell someone. I don't know you really. I mean, I didn't know you. You mean nothing to me, so why not tell you?

I heard her quick footsteps. She cried out loud in fake amazement: "Ashraf!"

I looked at her. I didn't move. I was sitting cross-legged on the comfortable chair, and I said coldly, "Lubna." She sat beside me on the floor and said with childlike enthusiasm, "Ashraf! Here in California! Ashraf, of course I should have expected it. Come with me."

I smiled my old smile, highly impressed by her energy. "Where to?"

She grabbed me by the hand and dragged me as she stood up. "Come with me, Ashraf. We will go around together."

I rose, perplexed. She hailed a taxi, saying in English, "Just drive around for an hour or two."

Then she opened the door and sat beside the driver. I smiled sarcastically. There were still traces of her communist tendencies.

"Are you not sitting next to me?"

"No, of course not. I will not sit next to you. First, I see no reason to erect a barrier between myself and the driver. We are equals. We are all equals."

"What are you doing in America, Lubna?" I said, laughing.

"A long story. Why did you give that sum of money to my brother? As revenge against me?"

"Maybe. What did he do with the money?" I said after a short pause.

"He got married with the money."

"I thought he would start a project."

"He did start a project, a marriage project, that survived for one year or two. Now he is unemployed, totally dependent on me, as usual."

"Why are you sitting next to the driver, Lubna?"

"I am afraid of you, Ashraf," she said as she got out a cigarette and started to smoke.

The driver motioned to her to stop smoking and showed her the notice, "No smoking."

She screamed in English, "As long as I pay you, I call the shots. I make the rules. Stop here! I want to sit in the backseat."

I laughed heartily as I saw my sweetheart adopting a cause that she did not comprehend. Believing in something and its opposite at one and the same time, and deceiving herself only to get angry at everything. In her words, I heard America speaking.

The car stopped. She got out and sat next to me. She moved closer and whispered, "Married, Ashraf?"

"Are you asking me or making a confession?"

"A confession. I married my comrade—remember him? The Iraqi journalist. The first man in my life."

"Here in America?" I looked at her in amazement.

"He wants to change everything. He has the same fury as myself, the same . . . you know, Ashraf, the conditions in Iraq. My husband suffered for years. He was severely tortured in prison. They killed his mother. Can you believe it? Security men forced their way into his house looking for him, after his release from prison. When they could not find him, they killed his mother. Of course, he hates the regime and those responsible. It is a barbaric, unjust regime. Didn't I tell you that before? He came out of prison unrecognizable. Muhannad, my husband, will make a difference. He will change things. He is hope for tomorrow. He will return to Iraq and play an important role there. He deserves it after all his suffering. Do you know what I mean?"

"No."

"The most important thing in life is freedom of expression, whether in a democracy or a communist country. What matters is freedom," she said looking briefly at me.

"The most important thing in life is to have your daily sustenance. Money, Lubna, creates wonders," I said, smiling.

"And how are you, Ashraf? Have you gotten married?"

I shook my head and said confidently, "I am well. I work in Virginia. And you?"

"I live with my husband. I am studying for my doctorate degree in Middle Eastern studies. One day . . ."

"I don't want to know. Happy?" I said, sounding bored and feeling furious.

"Of course not. I have never been happy. Not yet. The Arab world's concerns pain me," she said in her usual lively manner.

I touched her hand, and she said somewhat sarcastically, "Don't do that, please."

"You are now in America. What concern is the Arab world to you?"

"You don't understand me. Our world never escapes my mind. I think about Mother, and my brother. I think about our road in Imbaba, the state of our old building, and neighbors, and also the ideas . . ."

"Enough of this nonsense. You want to convince me you are still a communist, here in America."

"I still believe in equality, and I hate injustice. I will fight injustice and money as long as I live. Yes, I am a communist, if that's what you're asking," she said in anger.

"Are you deceiving me or deceiving yourself? Such naïveté! What are you doing here, exactly?" I said it through a dry laugh.

"I fight for freedom. Even if I do not like the regime here, I will exploit it to reach my end: freedom. I look forward to a day when I can shout aloud whatever I want without ending up in jail in one country or another, just because I dare to think."

"Poor you, Lubna." I was being sarcastic. "You are exploiting this regime? Is that what you've convinced yourself you're doing? They will exploit you, your husband, your family, your father and your mother as well! Oh, Lubna! You are so naïve. Or are you just trying to convince me? Or is it that you have become a slave of luxury, consumption, bananas, pistachios, and caviar?"

I knew she would get angry. I expected her familiar explosion. But she did not get angry, nor did she explode. She was suddenly silent. Pain was revealed through her eyes. She moved closer and kissed my cheek tenderly with her eyes closed and said, "I regretted it, Ashraf. I regretted it. I was young and was seized with anger."

Her lips on my cheek were soft, wet, and warm—the warmth of the neck of a chicken just slaughtered. She was warm. I missed her and feel jealous for her and fear her. She ignited a fire inside me that I thought had extinguished itself and died out a long time ago. She was a mixture of warmth, fury, despair, bitterness, naïveté, and violence.

Oh, Lubna, what have you done to me and to yourself?

I said no more.

I rested my head against the back of the seat, breathing slowly. I was not aware whether I was alive or dead, and with eyes closed I said, "I can see you, Lubna, as a university lecturer here in California. I can see you trembling as you talked about the Middle East problems. I can see tears in your eyes in your exile, while I can see also your big Mercedes car, its chauffeur, and your distinguished politician of a husband bringing freedom to his country. I can see you and can see me and feel regret. I don't know why life has done this to us."

"And what has life done to you?"

"Nothing. The problem is that life has done nothing to me or for me."

She looked at the cab's meter and asked the driver to return to the hotel.

"A thief. They swallow money here like we used to swallow Eid festival sweets. Do you intend to stay here, then, Ashraf?"

"I don't know. Let's talk about something other than you and me. Do you eat pistachios now? The American pistachios?"

She laughed, then suddenly said with her eyes overflowing with tears, "I want a child, Ashraf. I married him because I want a child."

"And him?"

"He wants a child. And you?"

Her questions embarrassed me. There was one single thing I could not handle, and that was Lubna knowing my current situation. Anything but that.

I looked at my watch and got out of the car, saying, "I'm sure I will soon see you with a child, and I will meet your husband."

"No problem. Are you going to pay the taxi, at least?" she cried as she got out of the car.

I laughed, emptying my pockets, "At least one day I'll feel that I paid for something for you."

She looked at me for a long moment and whispered, "Ashraf." Then she cried in anger, "How dare you leave me? Traitor!"

I looked at her, speechless. She vanished in seconds, driven by anger. Women!

Women are deep. They look at you with a different perspective. Who said women are trivial? Who said women are artificial? No. Women look at your insides and see the folds of your bank account.

Wafaa, I have never felt an urge to cry like I felt that day. I felt jealous of Lubna's husband. I felt envious of Lubna, and hated the whole world. I sat in my hotel room, closed the door, and looked at my palm. I am forty years old. I have achieved nothing. I may not become rich again, ever! I am working in a bank, the same job I had done when I was twenty-seven years old. Then I was a financial consultant in a big British bank. Now I work as a cashier in an American bank. I am now like an airport. Money passes through my hands like planes. They do not end there. I am the means, not the end. I am nothing. How I pity airports, and how I pity myself.

Well. Self-pity has never been my way. I will return richer than I was. Don't think I can't do it now, illegally. But I'm not used to that. I think the whole thing is a question of habit. If you are used to theft, you are then an expert in theft. If you are used to riches, you are rich. I am not used to thieving. But I am used to being rich.

I wiped a tear from my face. I left home and went to Amanda's. Have I talked to you about Amanda? It doesn't matter. She is like me, broken midway. She could not continue the journey. A single unmarried mother. She has a baby and an old car. She works as a secretary in the bank. I had been thinking about her. As soon as I returned, I headed for her place. I drowned my despair in hers. We said nothing to one another. She will not understand me, and I will not understand her. She needed me as I needed her. Meanwhile, Lubna never left my mind.

The problem was that I had met Lubna at the heat of youth. She rejected me and slapped my pride in the face. Had we met for the first time now, I might have been less arrogant and a lot wiser. I would have tried more than once, and she would have consented, I believe.

Fortune is silly. She left me because I was a capitalist. Now she is singing the praise of capitalism in the land of money and dreams. Here she is now eating pistachios with breakfast, lunch, and dinner. If only she had consented! If only we could turn back time! Would I love her after all this time? Maybe yes, maybe no. If I lived with her, I would have grown bored, just as I grew bored with everything, and just as I got bored with many women. But now I look at her with fury and hatred and wish she would drown in riches and luxury so that I might look at her and laugh at the principles she was once prepared to die for.

There is no principle, Wafaa, worth dying for. What we believe in today we forget tomorrow. Politics does not create life. Look at the world around you. Look at the wars and the blood. What is behind all these wars? Do you think principles and differences of religion, and cultures, etc., etc., are the reason? No. The reason behind wars is money. Greed and money. Freedom and tolerance and patience are qualities that are produced only by money. Money is the root of all evil, and I look forward desperately to having it.

That was the longest letter I have ever received from Ashraf. He might have written it in installments. I probably felt a tinge of jealousy of Lubna or Amanda or others, but it was mild jealousy. My jealousy could not match my pride. He was speaking to me. Me. He wanted to tell all to me. I was his only friend. I was the bucket into which he poured his feelings. How I loved being a bucket!

∾

Back to Lubna Thaabit.

Are power and the pursuit of power what killed Lubna's communism? Or was it despair and age? When had Muhannad returned to her life?

He was her first man. He was full of anger, while she was full of despair. He still wanted her, for his life was torn to pieces by various prisons and angry pamphlets. He wanted to rule his country. Who is better suited for that role than one who has suffered from a regime? He hoped he would be the one to mount the coup d'état. He was lucky to escape death. She met him and compared him to Ashraf. While her heart pounded for Ashraf and her body melted for his touch, her mind was with Muhannad. His ambition tempted her more than Ashraf's pistachios. She was infatuated with political power and coup d'états. She saw herself deciding the fate of people while she stood between her baby and Muhannad. She wished for a child who would not smell the stench of sewage every morning.

But why now? Was Lubna that stupid? If she had to abandon her beliefs and principles, why now?

The answer was that she wanted political power and military coups. She didn't want just money. Ashraf had offered to make her a princess in the British fashion, without a voice and without political views. As for Muhannad, he offered her a fight in order to be a leader. There was no comparison between the two offers.

Her baby was screaming to come out of her womb. He was not out yet. But he would be born in America to lead the struggle against injustice.

∿

Women! How wretched and how miserable! I pity women, and Lubna in particular. A woman never forgets a man she had made love to, ever. While she never forgot Muhannad when she was with Ashraf, Ashraf was in control of all her senses. Now that Muhannad was back, Ashraf remained in her memory. The comparison was not flattering to Muhannad, Ashraf, or Lubna herself. That was because Lubna had not been endowed with my imagination. Ashraf's touches would vanish from her memory the way corpses vanish in the theater of war.

I know that was what saddened her. Her treacherous memory.

∿

Events were happening all around me.

Spilling blood became a fact of daily life everywhere. But I had no interest in politics. My dream had not been to experience the taste of bananas. My dream was him.

The invasion of Kuwait and the war in Iraq were of no interest to me. Then he wrote again.

I suppose that there are limits to the deviations of people. With despair and fear all boundaries vanish. Today I severed my relation with Amanda. I couldn't take it anymore. There are limits to what people may do, even in moments of despair. Her room was small. She has three children. She had no problem kissing me and hugging me in front of them. I didn't mind. She used to visit me at my small apartment, leaving her children with the babysitter. But when I came today to take her to my apartment, she was crying, burying her face in her hands. She said she has been fired and that she is desperate and lonely and needs me.

She said she could not come with me, as the babysitter would not come today or tomorrow, because she cannot pay her. She looked at me hopefully and whispered, "Hold me, Ashraf. I want you badly."

I hugged her intensely as I looked at her children, who were watching TV indifferently.

She started kissing me, but I whispered, "Amanda! Your children!"

"What can I do? I have this room only. You know I can't leave them alone. Do you want me buried alive?"

"I will stay for a while, then I will leave. Tomorrow."

I said it firmly, but she came closer, "I want you, Ashraf!"

"And your children? Are you crazy?"

She moved away angrily, "You don't want me anymore. You are like all of them. Who wants a mother of three? Who will stand me?"

"Your children are with us in the room. Do you not notice that?" I whispered.

She noticed nothing. She was desperate. What she noticed were fear of the future, despair, and the abject poverty in which she is living.

She came closer again and began to unbutton my shirt.

I shouted, "You can't do that!"

"Don't you want me?" she asked miserably.

"No. I don't want you. Not now," I said cruelly.

I did not want her. I lost respect for her. I felt no pity toward her, for I was extremely angry. I left her place in anger, and when I arrived home I felt a mixture of pity, fear, and despair.

I sighed, and I wrote to him: *I love you.*
His wry reply arrived: *That's what you always say.*
Then I wrote him again:

I pity Amanda, Ashraf, and I pity my sister, Sally, and blame her as well. Humans are always like that; one wants something in particular and forgets all the beautiful things around him, and does not count the blessings. My sister has a beautiful baby boy. What does she do? She ignores him and treats him like a burden or a disaster that fate has piled on her back. Amanda thinks the same way. Life may offer them a fair deal in the future. But why do we use excessive injustice against those around us after we have tasted the bitterness of injustice ourselves? I don't know. I can't look my sister in the eye. Excuse me, Ashraf. I vowed to myself once that I would never hasten to judge others, but I never forgive those who are cruel, even if their cruelty comes at times of panic and despair.

I, for instance, imagine myself in Sally's place. If, for instance, I married you and, God forbid, you died, what would I do? If fate left part of you alive, I would keep it nearest to my heart. But I am romantic, as you know.

I almost saw his smile on reading the letter.
And his reply came:

Your imagination stuns and surprises me: I married you and died as well. Oh, my God! How I fear you, Wafaa! But I cannot force myself not to admire this wit and intelligence, which are revealed all of a sudden together with the contemplations and analysis! Is it your unique experience with your mother, your sister, and those around you? Or is it me who hurt you, unintentionally of course!

Let me tell you the truth for once. I thought you were the most stupid woman I had ever laid eyes on. There is nothing I hate in women more than stupidity. A stupid woman is capable of extinguishing any ray of hope within a man and of making him wish he were dead. But now I do not see you as stupid, Wafaa. I have not seen you as someone stupid for some time, since you sent me a letter, which I do not remember very well, where you stated strongly that you would live, whether I am in your life or not. Do you remember?

He wrote frequently, and I replied every time. I don't know whether he used to hate me then began to love me, or whether he used to despise me and had later come to respect me. Who had changed? I, he, or both of us? Why was he sending me letters? Was it my persistence, or was it just fate giving me a last chance? Did he pity me? What did he expect from me? What did he want, and was there a reason for everything?

It seemed to me that fate loves surprises, and that we lose a lot while we're busy swallowing fate's surprises. Every one of us has an impossible dream. My dream was sustaining me. He nourishes it with his letters.

Ashraf still pities airports as places that never became an end in themselves. He has become an airport, himself, carrying airplanes and remaining still, never flying high in the sky! Years ago he said, "How I pity airports." He said it again. It seemed to me the world could be divided into airports and airplanes. No more.

I felt the urge to write to him every day. He wrote me a letter every day, always short. They were always on a specific subject. I would write to him, *I love you,* and he would reply, *The quality of food in America is worthy of pity.*

The Ashraf of my dreams was different. During the last ten years my imagination had developed and matured. Ashraf no longer held my arm and proclaimed: "You cannot leave home today! You are mine! Do you understand? I don't want you to work! I don't want you to look at any man but me!"

The Ashraf of my present dreams was warm and affectionate. He would inundate me with emotions, not melt me altogether. He would hold me in his arms every day. His touches were tender. He was proud of me and of my achievements. He was proud of my private tutoring and my daily travel from Damanhour to Alexandria, and of the way I treated my adolescent pupils.

Yes, he was a figment of my imagination. He was now not as strong and solid as steel. He was no longer the rock that would support me, as he used to be in my imagination of ten years ago. I had come to be his rock, occasionally, as he had been mine. I saw him as vulnerable and human, and as a result I loved him even more.

Yes, he was a figment of my imagination. He might not know me well enough.

Despite that, he was with me every moment. He became the cup of tea I take every morning before going to work. As for him, I imagined that I had become the black coffee he drank every morning.

He was my friend; I was his. Our relationship was strange. It was not ideal. Is there an ideal relationship?

He once wrote: *What do you think about the color white? I imagine it to be the color used by those who have no history. Those who have history do not like the color white in buildings.*

I smiled and wrote back: *What color do we use in Egypt?*

His reply came a week later: *The color yellow.*

I hadn't tried to contact him by phone; I hadn't tried to hear his voice. He didn't give me his number, and I didn't ask for it. I feared speaking to him on the phone in case I went dumb. However, his voice had never left my ear, and time flies fast.

Then he wrote:

Dear Wafaa,

Have you seen the TV or read the papers? The invasion of Kuwait. I laughed on reading the news. Did I not say money makes miracles? I wonder when Lubna's husband is going to be a minister in a new Iraqi government, taking his orders from pistachio growers and sellers? In a year? Or thirteen years? One day Muhannad will return to Iraq and, with him, Lubna. I know, Wafaa. Well, we will not talk about politics. Let us talk about you. When are you going to get married? Are you not looking forward to having a baby?

Talk to me about yourself. What is it you want exactly, Wafaa?

What was it I want? He knew, and I knew that he knew. I don't know whether the question was for him to make sure or a wild emotional utterance influenced by the climate of crazy circumstances all around us. I expected Lubna's husband to be a minister in the future. I could imagine Lubna in expensive designer clothes sitting side-by-side with the American and the British, old and new colonials, eating nothing but pistachios and speaking in the name of the new masters. She would be eating bananas to the point of stomachaches and selling and buying pistachios.

I had no idea whether Lubna had conceded her defeat and surrendered, or whether in the heat of her fury she was fighting everything and anything. But she'd left Ashraf because of pistachios, because he used to eat them. She didn't realize that she would end up selling pistachios and being devoured by them. To me, pistachios seem to be a magic potion that will strike some people down with a curse and endow others with happiness to the fullest.

I began to feel that the solution was in pistachio nuts. But my mind could not yet come up with the formula. How could I make my dreams a reality? How would Ashraf return to me? On its own, love would not bring him back. My romantic and naïve ideas would not bring him back. I had to seek help from pistachios. God exists; may he help me.

He wrote:

Wafaa,

I cried again.

I cried for a whole hour or maybe less. I'm not ashamed of that. Why should I be? What have I done to make me ashamed? The cave was closed, and I was inside after the whole treasure had been stolen. I was all alone, and the cave was extremely small.

I am in the midst of the biggest consumer society. But I see nothing in it except the stench of toilets. Everything is abundantly available in America: food, electronic appliances, even human goods, fatal gaiety, and destructive despair. It is a dense country.

What is the news of Egypt? Has it changed, Wafaa?

That day I felt a rage and impatience so I wrote to him: *What will you do if I get married?? I can get married. Do you know that? Who is going to speak to you then?*

I regretted writing it. It was hysterical and infantile and did not answer his question about the state of Egypt.

His reply came a few days later: *How are you, Wafaa? I'm afraid I can't answer your question. Excuse me, for I don't answer hypothetical questions. You are not married, and thank God for that.*

"Thank God for that"! That was all he said. What did it mean? What did he expect? Did he expect me to be overjoyed with this reply? Or did he expect me to be sad? He did say "Thank God," didn't he?

With my mind's eye I could see many images. An image for each country. An image linked in my mind to Ashraf and his words, spoken or written.

I used to see Britain as dark green, with ancient houses and heavy rain falling into a huge sewer, endlessly. I would hear the monotonous sound of falling water. In the dark street I would see the corpse of Dr. Mahmoud Daawood, Ashraf's father, by the sewer. His blood mixing with the rainwater . . . I would smell fresh rainwater mixed with dried blood. That was Britain.

As for America, I used to see it with the eyes of Ashraf: I saw the filthy white toilet, the vomit, the tissue, the big cake with cinnamon and burnt sugar. I would see Ashraf in the midst of huge crowds who stampeded to buy the cake while he stood aloof, lost and frustrated. He had no money for the cake with the cinnamon and sugar. That was America.

In my mind the image of Egypt was that of Aunt Aliyya sitting on the gold-colored couch in the middle of the living room. In her hand were many tablecloths. I would also smell incense mixed with the smells of mothballs, and yesterday's cooking. That was Egypt.

All day long I thought about nothing except pistachio nuts, especially the two I saw in Ashraf's pocket the day I fell in love with him. The pistachios never left my mind. I didn't know how I could benefit from it, or how I might break out of my passivity as I demolished the fear that was gripping my insides.

I did not write to him about it. I was merely thinking, with my imagination growing wilder and wilder.

And then he wrote:

Dear Wafaa,

Today I have obtained my American passport. It is here in my pocket. I have become an American. I don't know what this means. It seems that I have just become responsible for all the woes and wealth of mankind. I am now hated by many, and feared by more. Everyone will bow in respect to me. I may one day be stabbed with a jagged edge because I am an American. I fear daggers. I will wave my hand, and car doors and state borders will be opened for me. My point of view will be in all the papers.

My name will be a household word.

I have an American passport. Though I have not killed even an ant or trespassed on a house, I will be accused of being responsible for all the massacres and all the dead. I may be killed for an act committed by the American administration. Many crimes will be committed in my name, and in my name also many borders between states will just vanish.

What is there in a passport?

And who am I?

Am I a mere passport? Is man reduced to a document made out of cheap paper and bad ink?

Is that me?

Everyone looks at my passport, but no one wants to know who I am.

A small card, of course, and no more. A small card and a bundle of bones and blood, no more. If I die, people may see me as yet another American who has just died. Some may even rejoice. Some may wage wars in my name. Some of these wars may be for me; others may be against.

Who am I, Wafaa?

Egyptian? What does that mean?

Just a feeling. A word, no more. Why do you love me? Just so. No reason whatsoever. Why do I feel Egyptian? It is just so: no reason whatsoever.

I lived in Britain, rich and spoiled for thirty years, but I never felt British. I lived in America for eight years in abject poverty, lodging in the wretched quarters of the very poor. I never felt American.

I lived in Egypt for a few months. I had seen Egypt in Mother's tears and Father's arrogance, in the songs of Abdalhaleem Haafiz and Umm Kulthoum. It was in you, in Lubna, in Aunt, in Sally and Kareem, in socializing and in weddings. I used to look at you through my window with snobbery. Still, I would feel I was nothing. That feeling crept into me gradually with the mixture of dreams, despair, impotence, dignity, and sadness.

Before Lubna, I had a feeling of arrogance, pride, vanity, fear, and poverty. But my biggest fear was if my truth was revealed. I have collected passports as some collect butterflies. But I am seized by a feeling that I am an Egyptian, just so, for no reason whatsoever.

I slept holding the letter to my bosom. I felt relieved and full of hope, dreaming about the pistachios and what I could do.

When I finished the last of my private lessons on the modern history of Egypt, I wrote a letter to Ashraf, as I did every day.

You have asked me before about the conditions in Egypt. Things are fine. We now use e-mail. All our schools have computers, at least one for each school. People buy computers. Some don't use them. We have many shopping centers and malls—did you know that? The international brands and names are here: "Bali" for shoes, "Chanel" and "Christian Dior" for clothes and cosmetics. We now enjoy our evenings touring these malls and shopping centers. We have become an advanced and modern country.

Oh, I forgot—we now have Chinese restaurants as well. Can you see how tolerant and progressive and what believers of equality we have become? We have come to respect other cultures and appreciate them, including sampling various cuisines, even the Japanese "sushi."

You have asked me about how Egypt is doing. Egypt has an open door for everyone who contributes to the development and progress plan. In fact, there is a remarkable development in manufacturing, especially the manufacture of fine chocolate.

You have asked me about how Egypt is doing. We are in the mid-nineties. I expect a major leap forward by the next ten years. I expect that every Egyptian baby will have a pacifier and a milk bottle both made in America. Instead of Egyptian fathers coming home carrying watermelons, or a bag of Jawava, they now carry hamburger meals with toys made in China. We will abandon all backward customs like the sweet sugar dolls for the birthday of the Prophet, and the cakes of the Eid festival and so on. We will replace all of these with Italian ice cream, French pastries, and Dutch sweets.

We are in the mid-nineties. I wish you were here, Ashraf. I wish you could see the changes that have taken place in our country, the changes in us and in the cooperatives, making the word obsolete, used only by grandparents when hallucinating.

Egypt is standing at the threshold of a new era. Remember these words in a decade's time when international security and peace prevail.

When Iraq is liberated.

When Aunt Aliyya becomes famous, and her ideas on the punishment and torture of the dead in their graveyards get to be written on every wall, when Egyptians eat Chinese and call for the six principles of the revolution once more.

Remember these words. Try to understand that Egypt is now ready for pistachios.

Well. Who are we, Ashraf?

While I was teaching the modern history of Egypt today, I felt I have come to realize who we are.

We do not need to study all of the middle ages.

All we need is to study the history of pharaohs and modern history in order to understand who we are. Why have we built the pyramids, Ashraf? For the glory and immortality of our kings? Yes, and for our sake as well. When you look at the pyramids, you see the time, money, and lives exerted for the sake of constructing this huge monument for the purpose of glorifying ourselves. That's because we love vanity, boasting, and laughter. For this reason, after all the time you have spent in America, I advise you to return to Egypt. You can initiate a small project in which I can be a partner. It's a pistachio project: we import them from Iran, Syria, or America, or the three countries together. Then we sell them in Egypt. The rich and the poor will go for it, as they both love boasting and bragging. More pistachios than bread will be sold. That's because everyone eats bread, but only a privileged few appreciate pistachios. It will not remain a minority of a few privileged Egyptians. The Egyptians will stampede for pistachios as they do for cars, telephones, and computers. A house without pistachios will be like a house without gilt-covered furniture—that is to say, a house for the poor.

We Egyptians are like you, Ashraf: we hate and fear poverty, but he who fears demons ends up seeing them—for years I have been thinking about this. For years I have been waiting for you, to get married to you, but you were not interested. Thirteen years later you are now in love with me. Is that not so?

I used pistachios to entice him, as a wave attracts the sand. I had to think, and I used pistachios. That's how everyone does it. I felt a strange serenity and happiness. I knew the result beforehand.

A Passport

Each age requires a different passport, and each country has a different feel.

—Ashraf Daawood

7

Cairo International Airport, 1993

Ashraf looked at his Egyptian passport and then at his American passport and pondered which one to choose. He looked at the two lines, the one for Egyptians, and the other for non-Egyptians. The line for the non-Egyptians was shorter. He took out his American passport and presented it. Every era has its passport, and every country has its special taste. Every country has a different feel. Today, carrying his American passport, he felt more Egyptian than he ever had before.

Why did he feel he was Egyptian? What does that feeling mean? He didn't know. He felt an urge to close his eyes and sleep. He might wake up to curse past years and curse these people. But what he wanted now was to sleep, just to sleep. Despite the fact that the flight back had been long, he hadn't slept on the plane.

~

I extended my hand with confidence and yearning, the yearning of thirteen years of waiting. I didn't look at him. I wanted to shake hands with him. I stole a glance or two at him. He looked different. He had some wrinkles; his hair had some gray in it. He seemed different from the youth he had been, who had never left my memory. He might have stolen a glance or two at me as well. I was different, naturally. He looked at me and compared my past looks to my present looks. My hair was in a ponytail, and I wore no makeup. I was wearing a white blouse and a black skirt to reveal my slim figure, and a pair of black shoes, which had lost their original color thanks to Cairo's dust and had become a mixture of gray and black. They were high heels and a bit too tight. I regretted wearing them. I had polished my nails and visited the hair salon. However, I could not let my hair loose before him. So I stood like an idiot—embarrassed, shy, and extremely happy.

It was a strange situation. However, he knew everything about me, and I knew everything about him. We walked side-by-side in silence. His seriousness stunned me. His fixed gaze that penetrated nothing puzzled me. He might have found the situation strange. I couldn't tell. Each of us knew the other by heart.

"We'll take the train to Damanhour," I said, trying to overcome my embarrassment.

"And the pistachios? Our project?" He smiled.

"We'll talk on the train."

He nodded.

"A good decision," I said enthusiastically.

He looked at me and smiled his familiar smile. "You have changed a bit, Wafaa, but you are still . . . how can I describe you . . . ?"

"Naïve and absent-minded?" I said.

"Never. You are still young. I like the youthful look that has not left your eyes," he added.

I was feeling a mixture of tension, excitement, gaiety, and anxiety. This was what I had dreamed of all my life. The moment I saw him, my mind froze, as if it had performed its last assignment.

I was at a loss for words all of a sudden. I had a lot to say, but I forgot everything and focused my attention on his shoulder, which almost touched mine but didn't. As had always been the case with Ashraf, things would *nearly* happen all the time. The nearer hope approaches, the sooner it flees, like a skillful mouse. But this time I was holding fast to hope. I had chained it with iron fetters behind the bars of my imagination.

I looked at his hand tapping his thigh nervously, as if he was experiencing a mixture of instability, fear, pain, frustration, and strange satisfaction. What would happen now if I put my hand on his? Here I was attending to details, once more. So I closed my eyes and whispered, "Ashraf."

"Yes?" he said, as he stared through the window at the expanse of plantations along the track.

"Do you know what I have in mind?" I asked without thinking.

Without looking at me, he smiled and said, "I have no idea. Your imagination follows no rules. Your imagination, cousin, is wild."

"I used to dream about you when I was young. Did you know that? I used to have dreams . . ." I fell silent.

"What dreams?" He glanced at me.

"You know—adolescent dreams, but not petty ones. They were never petty dreams at all. They were just daring," I said, rebuking him.

Faking surprise, he said apprehensively, "Daring?"

"Very daring indeed," I said energetically. "I will tell you about them one day. Do you want to know about them, Ashraf?"

He was silent for a few seconds. Then he looked at me with sadness and then tenderness in his eyes. "Of course I want to know about them."

"In Damanhour I'll tell you about it in detail," I said excitedly.

"With all the details. The minute details," he said gently.

I didn't want to say anymore. How beautiful pistachios were! They made miracles. Pistachios, in addition to my active imagination. He closed his eyes, and we both fell silent.

⌁

At the Damanhour train station Ashraf stood for a while, recalling old memories. The shantytown dwellings had not changed. The pastry seller was still there, but not the liver-selling place. He couldn't tell whether that meant that stray animals had vanished from Egypt or if Egyptians were boycotting liver for one reason or another, perhaps because it was being imported from the countries of the new colonials. Or was it simply because the owner of the place was no longer alive or might have moved into a bigger place in a different location?

Ashraf stared at the wide stairs of the station, remembering the fat woman who used to sit in front of her cottage near the station, screaming proudly at her children, cursing and insulting them, and then sweeping the floor, without any feelings or emotions on her face.

⌁

I hailed a taxi.

His eyes were fixed on the grocery store with the white teddy bears that carried red hearts and English proverbs and phrases about love—as if love in the English language was no longer a disgrace, although in Arabic it still was. All the love words written on the teddy bears were in English. He smiled once more.

We rode together. The driver was a middle-aged man. He had a gloomy face, and his car was full of blue beads. He was listening to a song by Mohammed Tharwat:

Beware of my heart when you greet me
Beware of my heart, beware
For my heart is in my hands.

"What is the problem here if a man shakes hands with a woman?" Ashraf asked. "How fixated with details are Egyptians! What's wrong with a look or with shaking hands? What's wrong with a hug or a kiss? Nothing. It doesn't mean anything anywhere else. But in Egypt, every move has a meaning. Every look has a meaning. We love details. Isn't that so, Wafaa?"

"We love details," I replied. "What Mother cooked, how many spoons of ghee on the okra today, what my sister bought today, and does she have gilt furniture in her sitting room? Does she have curtains with or without fringe? . . . And the tablecloth, is it ornate or plain? And the chandelier, is it crystal or glass . . . ? Et cetera, et cetera."

"You have changed, cousin." He looked at me with a smile, but I made no reply.

I felt an unusual optimism and love for Damanhour: The shantytown cottages, the houses, the large shop signs, and the streets, which were half rural and half urban.

I was from Damanhour. I was reserved and thirty-three years old. I feared the passage of time. I was somewhat stupid, but somewhat clever as well. I was somewhat timid, and somewhat direct and daring. In that particular moment I was in love. The singer Mohammed Tharwat and the music of Egypt—its noise, weddings, and love—overwhelmed me. I could hardly control my nerves.

The pastry seller and the kebab vender looked at me reassuringly, so I whispered confidently, "Egypt is now ready for pistachios."

～

He inspected the living room as soon as we walked in. He found it as it had been; no change, though Mother used to promise every year that she would redecorate it soon.

The moment she set eyes on him, Mother hugged him and kissed him, many strong and violent kisses, crying, "Ashraf! My darling! How are you, darling?"

He was staring at my hair, and at my new glasses, and the many teacher workbooks that litter our dining-room table.

Kareem hugged him and shook hands with him. Kareem loved money and hated poverty. All he ever hoped for was to marry a rich girl who owned an apartment. That hope had not been realized yet.

Sally entered the room enthusiastically, screaming, "Ashraf!"

Did she hug him? Did she?

Yes. It seemed so. She had changed. She had put on some weight and was full of femininity and womanliness.

I envied her once more. But I had already decided that he would hug me, one day soon.

She sighed as she sat beside him and said in a mixture of coquetry and sadness, "Have you heard what has happened to your cousin, Ashraf?" (Meaning herself.) "Catastrophes, catastrophes!"

He nodded, saying nothing. So she added as she looked at him suddenly, "But you're still handsome. You still wear your jeans well."

"Necessity is the mother of invention." He smiled sarcastically.

"I'd marry you now, Ashraf, but I'm already married. I wish I had known that you would come back. How did you come?"

He rested his head on the back of the chair, saying nothing. He was just looking at his aunt as she sat in the lounge chair. Her husband had squeezed himself beside her. In front of them was a small table with a large tray, carrying plates of rice, parsley, tomatoes, and a pot of cabbage leaves. She said energetically, "I will soon make the stuffed cabbage that you love, darling."

The inside walls were still dirty. The embroidered tablecloth was still there. Everything was as it had been thirteen years ago.

Except for the people. Misery shadowed their eyes. Their features were accurate testimonies of age.

He sat beside me and said seriously, "Let's talk about the project."

I nodded.

"Here or in the dining room?" he asked, businesslike again.

"Here," I said, picking up some teacher workbooks by way of support.

He sat down on the sofa and stretched out his arms.

I closed the door. There was something I missed about him. He was different, serious. Yes, the problem was that he was serious. I was used to seeing him tender and playful. I was not used to him being so serious.

He used to love games, adventures, and fooling around. I missed all that. These qualities were what had attracted me to him.

I whispered, as if pricking him, in order to wake him up. "Are you going to confess today or tomorrow?"

"Are there martial laws, still, in Egypt?" he said, smiling.

"What do you mean?"

"What are you going to do to me, Wafaa, to get me to confess? Torture me? Did I not tell you before that a confession under torture loses its halo, like getting high marks by cheating?"

"Getting high marks is sufficient. The means do not concern me. Anyone hearing you speaking like that would think that your life was a model of honor."

He raised his eyebrows, astonished and rather angry. "You have become very daring and forward. Is this a criticism, Wafaa? Have we not come here to talk about the project? Have I traveled all this distance to have a quarrel with you?"

"I just miss your laughter," I said tenderly, swallowing hard.

"I'm not going to laugh now. Maybe if I become rich again, one day."

"And if not?"

"I won't laugh. Let's talk about pistachios." He was almost impatient.

"Let me have the confession first!"

He smiled, heaving a deep sigh. "Didn't I tell you that confession this way is no victory? I hate prison, torture, detention centers, and women who are as persistent as jailers."

Faking indifference, I asked, "Don't you want to know first what I would like you to confess?"

He rose, laughing. "You want to dictate the confession as well. Wafaa, I'm tired. I want to go to bed. We'll talk tomorrow."

I didn't know whether he pitied himself as he entered the same house after all these years, and after he had lost everything.

Did I see any sadness in his eyes? Yes. A lot of that, together with gray hair, which had become more obvious now.

I whispered, hopefully, "You entered my room and touched me. Do you remember? You touched my cheek, neck, and arm. You said to me that love is beautiful. Do you remember? Confess, Ashraf! I am not imagining it. Tell the truth!"

He broke into a sudden fit of laughter, saying, "Oh, my God! Are you joking, Wafaa? Did I travel all this distance to tell you whether I had deceived you or not, touched you or not? Do you think I remember this incident? I forgot the secret account number, losing thousands of dollars. Do you think I will remember this incident?"

"But you remember. I know you remember," I said hopefully.

He looked me in the eye and smiled suddenly, the same smile I had missed and that betrayed the mischievousness of children and the naughtiness of adults. He whispered as he held the door, "Yes, I remember."

"You touched me and said the words."

"That didn't happen at all," he said innocently.

"Liar!"

"What about the pistachios?"

"Liar!"

"You know me. I love lying."

"You have not changed."

"A bit, perhaps."

I closed my eyes, took a deep breath, and whispered, "Can you hug me now, as you hugged Sally?"

He thought briefly, looked at me, smiled, and said, "Maybe. Why not?"

He opened his arms and said the sentence I had heard so often in my mind: "Come here."

I heard a knock on the door. My heart almost stopped as I called out, "Who?"

"It's me—Sally. The food is ready."

He smiled as he whispered, "Come here, Wafaa."

I covered the remaining step toward him. I placed my hand on his white shirt, and then on his chest, avoiding his eyes. I threw my head against his chest. He surrounded my waist with his arms. Yearning was exploding within me.

I whispered, "Is this an Egyptian or an American hug?" I wrapped my arms around him, whispering, "No one has ever hugged me except you."

"I pity you, Wafaa."

"Aren't you happy? You're the first and last man in my life!"

He held my arm saying, "Are you going to be like this for an hour?"

I said sadly, "You don't want me. You have to answer my question first."

He left me, returning to the sofa. His eyes were full of naughtiness, innocence, and mischief. He whispered, mockingly, stretching his arms on the back of the couch, "What was the question?"

"The hug," I said.

He gazed at my face for a second before saying, "I don't know. It was just a brief embrace. I haven't made up my mind."

Happiness shone in my eyes as I sat beside him, resting my head on his shoulder once more, easily and confidently. "Ashraf."

"An Egyptian hug, Wafaa."

"What does it mean?"

"I don't know. You tell me what it means."

"I never left you for a moment. Do you know the feeling—that though you have not seen someone for a long time, you still wish he was with you all the time?"

"How do you feel now?"

"I feel that innocent pistachio nuts are in my mouth, fresh and delicious. And you?"

He started stroking my hair, saying nothing. His touch was affectionate and tender. It was better than my dreams. I felt the throbbing of his heart and the warmth of his body. His grip on my shoulder was strong and confident. I didn't want to let go of him at all.

Sally knocked on the door again. "Ashraf, the food is getting cold."

"We're discussing the pistachios matter. Go ahead and start without us," he said in a businesslike manner.

"Don't leave me again, ever," I whispered, holding his hand.

"I didn't leave you, Wafaa," he protested.

"But you left."

"There was nothing between us for me to leave you. Do you know what I mean?"

"And now?" I asked angrily.

He pondered briefly and said, faking gloominess, "Now?"

"Now."

"I liked the Egyptian hug. You are affectionate, Wafaa. And gentle and sincere."

He stroked my cheek like he was demarcating my borders and identifying me, like he was drawing me in his imagination.

I closed my eyes. Was I dreaming? Did he say that?

"Ashraf, I have loved you all these years."

"Yes, I know," he smiled playfully.

"Will you marry me?"

"What is your threat this time?"

"Pistachios!"

"But I'm poor now. Don't you remember? I have no more than two thousand dollars to start the project. How can I get married? Let's wait till we start."

"We get married first," I interrupted him impatiently.

"Are you buying me as well? This is difficult, Wafaa."

"I have no money to buy you. If I had it, I would have paid millions of dollars to get you," I said angrily.

He sighed playfully, pushing me a bit in order to look into my eyes. His arm was still around my shoulder. "That much?"

"My share is time and effort. Yours, the capital."

"And then?"

"You marry me."

"And then?"

"We start the project."

"What if it fails?"

"Then we start another project. As long as our project is useful, it will succeed. Egyptians love useful projects like selling cars, telephones, pistachios, or imported cheese . . ."

"Where do we import the pistachios from?"

"Will you marry me?"

"Of course I'll marry you. Do I have any other choice?"

"You love me?"

"I need you."

"How?"

"I have needed you for all these years, to talk to you. I love talking to you. You sometimes provoke me, but I need you. Sometimes I would do something, or go somewhere, and say to myself, 'If Wafaa found out about that, she'd be upset, she'd cry, whatever' . . . I would tell myself that I should tell Wafaa, I should write to her about this or that. You were disturbing and challenging me all the time. I could not get you out of my mind."

"You love me, then?"

"Maybe. I have never analyzed my feelings."

"Whom do you love more: me or Lubna?"

"Back to the interrogation again!"

"I won't ask you. Let's talk about the pistachios. Where do you get them from?" I was a bit shaken.

"Iran, America, or Syria."

I pondered briefly. "Yes. Iran is an old country. Our relation with it has been cut for years. Perhaps if we open the door of commerce, we may help restore diplomatic relations and . . ."

But he interrupted me, "What concern is Iranian diplomatic relation to us? Politics again! Keep away from politics, Wafaa!"

"Well. What about Syria? It is an Arab sister state. Aleppo pistachios are unparalleled."

"Yes. True."

"But Iran has nuclear weapons, and it is a strong country," I said enthusiastically.

"And America?"

"Rich, and strong, and in control of the fate of mankind."

"Who?" Ashraf asked.

"America."

"What about the three countries together?"

I whispered as I laced my fingers with his, "Egypt is now ready for pistachios."

Author's Note

PLACES AND EVENTS in this story will be familiar to those familiar with Egypt, but they may be puzzling to American readers.

The name Sally is an Egyptian name as well as an English one (Nora is another). Sally's second marriage is a common-law marriage. Common-law marriages are usually secretive and not registered by the government and can be done privately with only two witnesses. Marital rights for women, such as the right of inheritance, are not guaranteed in such a marriage.

The story unfolds in Damanhour, a small town in the Behaira Province; in Alexandria; and in Cairo, where some of the characters live in the upper-class residential district of Zamalek and some in the poorer Imbaba district. There is also a scene in Muhandiseen, a rich quarter of Cairo popular with gulf Arabs and foreigners. Wafaa works in Alexandria, and some scenes take place in Sidi Jabir, an old quarter of that city, where the train station and the international call center are located.

Mention is made of a few popular artists of the time. Abdal-haleem Haafiz was a famous 1960s Egyptian singer who died in his forties. At least two women were reported to have committed suicide upon hearing the news of his death. The Egyptian singer Umm Kulthoum (1904–1975) was perhaps the most famous entertainer of the Arab world. One could compare her popularity to that of Elvis Presley. Mohammed Tharwat is a modern singer who comes from the provincial city of Tanta.

Readers might not be familiar with some aspects of Egyptian history. The Egyptian revolution took place on July 23, 1952. Three days later, the king was forced to abdicate and leave the country. Nasser took over power in 1954. Aunt Aliyya mentions "burying girls alive," which was a custom in pre-Islamic Egypt for poor families in Bedouin communities, who were afraid of the shame a girl would bring, especially because of poverty. The practice is explicitly forbidden in the Koran, and it ceased after the spread of Islam in the Arabian peninsula.

"Kassim" is the greedy brother in the traditional story English readers know as "Ali Baba and the Forty Thieves." In the story, Ali Baba opened the secret door of the cave by hearing the secret words said by the thieves. He then took some of the treasure inside the cave and left by uttering the secret words again. His brother Kassim tried to do the same, except he was too greedy and decided to take all the treasure. He died at the hands of the thieves. There are different versions of the story.

Jew's mallow is a green soup made with chicken or rabbit stock and a plant of the same name that is similar to spinach. It is a dish particular to Egypt.

Pistachios are the most expensive nuts in Egypt. They are usually exported from abroad. They were very rare in the 1980s when, after President Sadat's death in 1980, the Egyptian government banned imports. The aim of this ban was to change the open-door policy encouraged by Sadat. It was therefore a luxury to eat pistachios, offer them to guests, or cook with them. Nowadays, after the strong capitalism movement of the 1990s, pistachios in Egypt are not rare, but they are still very expensive.

Other titles from *Middle East Literature in Translation*

A Brave New Quest: 100 Modern Turkish Poems
    Talat S. Halman, trans. and ed., Jayne L. Warner, assoc. ed.

A Child from the Village
    Sayyid Qutb; John Calvert and William Shepard, eds. and trans.

Canceled Memories: A Novel
    Nazik Saba Yared

Contemporary Iraqi Fiction: An Anthology
    Shakir Mustafa, ed. and trans.

Distant Train: A Novel
    Ibrahim Abdel Megid; Hosam M. Aboul-Ela, trans.

I, *Anatolia and Other Plays: An Anthology of Modern Turkish Drama, Volume Two*
    Talat S. Halman and Jayne L. Warner, eds.

İbrahim the Mad and Other Plays: An Anthology of Modern Turkish Drama, Volume One
    Talat S. Halman and Jayne L. Warner, eds.

The Journals of Sarab Affan: A Novel
    Jabra Ibrahim Jabra; Ghassan Nasr, trans.

My Thousand and One Nights: A Novel of Mecca
    Raja Alem and Tom McDonough

Sleeping in the Forest: Stories and Poems
    Sait Faik; Talat S. Halman, ed., Jayne L. Warner, assoc. ed.

The Virgin of Solitude: A Novel
    Taghi Modarressi; Nasrin Rahimieh, trans.